PAGAN RITUAL!

In the center of the circle was a pagan altar much like the one Clint had seen earlier.

To the right of the altar a short man in a yellow shirt and torn pants banged hypnotically on his drum while the rest of the men took up a monotonous chant. Nearby, several women, a few of whom Clint recognized as being part of the castle staff, danced in a lusty frenzy to the beat, their mostly naked bodies shining with sweat and oils in the licking flame of the lanterns.

Finally, Clint returned his gaze to the altar. He looked closely at the naked female form resting there, apparently ready for sacrifice, as the women danced around it.

Then he realized why the form looked so familiar . . .

Don't miss any of the lusty, hard-riding action
in the Charter Western series, THE GUNSMITH

And coming next month:
THE GUNSMITH #59: THE TRAIL DRIVE WAR

THE GUNSMITH

58

THE DEADLY HEALER

J. R. ROBERTS

CHARTER BOOKS, NEW YORK

THE GUNSMITH #58: THE DEADLY HEALER

A Charter Book/published by arrangement with
the author

PRINTING HISTORY
Charter edition / October 1986

ISBN: 0-441-30962-3

Charter Books are published by The Berkley Publishing Group,
200 Madison Avenue, New York, New York 10016.
PRINTED IN THE UNITED STATES OF AMERICA

ONE

The Gunsmith was six miles outside Denver when the fanatic appeared in the middle of the road.

The fanatic wore a filthy piece of sackcloth and carried a long, knobby piece of wood meant to simulate a staff. His gray shoulder-length hair was nearly as filthy as his crude dress, and his bare feet were raw with open wounds.

"Praise ye, brother," he shouted up to Clint Adams. "You are on your way to see the man that God has brought as our salvation."

The fanatic would have been no more than mildly

1

amusing if his nose weren't running and his lips weren't bone-white with disease. Clint had recently read a New York newspaper article on insane asylums. Apparently the places were filled with unfortunates such as this man.

Clint reached inside his coat, found a gold eagle coin and tossed it down to the man.

"Thank you, brother," the man said, bending to pick up the coin. "Now I have something to offer up to the Reverend Wellfall."

"Why don't you use it for food and to see a doctor?" Clint said, nodding at the man's feet.

"I haven't made an offering in six days," the man explained. "How do you think the Reverend feels about that?" His tone implied that of the two of them, Clint was the one who was mad.

Clint thought a moment.

"I thought Jesus was partial to poor folks."

The man shook his head.

"Reverend Wellfall says that's a misinterpretation of the Holy Scripture."

It was easy to see that Clint could do nothing for the man.

He tightened up the reins, getting the wagon that was his combination home and gunsmith shop ready to travel again. In the mid-afternoon sunlight the team horses and Duke, his prize black gelding, stood poised to travel again.

"You're on to Denver, are you not?" the fanatic asked.

Clint nodded.

"Then you should visit the Reverend Wellfall yourself. He will help you."

Yes, Clint thought, he'll help me right out of my hard-earned money.

He had one more question for the fanatic.

"Do you live out here?"

The area looked empty of edible plants or anything resembling real shelter. Maybe there were caves in the nearby mountains.

"I want to be near the waters," the fanatic explained.

"What waters would those be?" Clint asked, frowning.

"Why, Reverend Wellfall's healing waters. People the world over come to be cleansed there." He indicated the open wounds on his feet. "Someday the waters will cleanse me, if only I can please the Reverend adequately."

Clint thought of telling the man about ministers such as this Wellfall but then thought better of it. Ultimately you could not talk anybody out of a deeply-held belief. They had to do that for themselves.

Clint dug into his pocket once again.

"I'll make you an offer."

"What's that?"

"You give the first gold coin to Reverend Wellfall, but this coin—" and he held it up so that it caught fire in the sunlight, "—this coin you'll keep for yourself."

"My stomach *could* do with some food," the man admitted.

"Then feed it," Clint said, and tossed the gold piece to the man, who caught it in midair this time.

"May God and the Reverend Wellfall bless you."

Clint smiled.

"I'll settle for God's blessing, if you don't mind."

With that he tightened the reins again and rode on into Denver.

TWO

Denver was one of Clint Adams' favorite cities. He agreed with whoever had called the place "a smaller New York." If anyone doubted that they had only to look at the Windsor Hotel.

The Windsor boasted 300 rooms, three elevators and gaslights in each room. There were even 60 bathtubs. Not to mention a ballroom the size of a substantial prairie and a swimming pool big enough to hold a dozen whales.

Clint had stayed in Denver once before, but he had not stayed at the Windsor. On that occasion he'd had to pay his own hotel bill. This time around his friend Jim West, of the United States Secret Service, had sent him a telegram asking him to travel at once to Denver and check into the Windsor, where he'd receive instructions on a case of grave importance to the country. Clint, while not noisy about his patriotism, felt he owed his country a great deal and so he accepted. The fact that the United States was picking up all of the bills only made the deal that much sweeter.

He only hoped that he'd be dealing with West himself this time and not his asshole boss, Fenton, as he had done in the past.

After finding a livery stable and a hostler to be trusted with his wagon and Duke, Clint walked back through the warm late afternoon to the Windsor.

The lobby of the place might have been in a European city.

Clint could not remember ever seeing so many fancy dressed people. Even men who looked to be doing little more than lounging were dressed up in Edwardian coats and shirts with frills. If they were this elegant during the afternoon, what would they look like at dinner time?

The desk clerk seemed disapproving. He developed a tiny frown and twitch in his lips as he watched Clint approach.

"May I . . . help you?"

Yeah, Clint thought, you'd like to help me right out onto the street, wouldn't you?

"A room, please."

"Do you have a reservation?"

Clint gave the man a broad, shit-eating grin. "Of course."

Doubtful, the man took Clint's name and looked up the reservation. It was obvious that he didn't expect to find it, but there it was, causing his frown to deepen.

But at this precise moment Clint didn't give a damn. Nor was he even paying attention. A beautiful distraction had come along.

He put her age at twenty, no more. She wore a corseted silk dress that matched the fabric of her parasol. She stood primly—making her all the more sexy— against one of the two grand stairways that seemed to sweep up to Heaven itself. Her high-buttoned shoes shone with the same intensity as the smile she visited on Clint.

"How about hurrying up? I'm in a hurry," Clint told the clerk.

The desk clerk followed Clint's gaze and then gave the Gunsmith a withering look. Look here, the clerk seemed to say, you do not accost attractive young females in the lobby of the Windsor Hotel.

"You have luggage?"

"Just these," Clint said, picking up his saddlebags. He had a canvas bag in his rig, but he'd chosen to leave it behind in favor of the saddlebags.

"I see. If you will wait a moment I'll have someone show you to your—"

"That's not necessary," Clint said. "Just give me the key and I'll find it myself."

"Of course."

Key in hand, saddlebags over his shoulder, Clint moved to the staircase and the beautiful brunette.

When he reached her she laughed and said, "You'd be the man I'm waiting for, I'll wager."

"How long have you been waiting?"

"It would sound pretty if I said all my life, wouldn't it?"

"Yes."

She smiled again.

"Unfortunately, 'tis only about twenty minutes that I have been standing here."

He laughed, too. He liked her beauty and humor and the hint of an Irish brogue.

"You're going to your room, I presume?" she asked.

He nodded.

"I'll wager there's a bath in there."

"That's another wager you'd win."

"And I'll also wager that you'll need someone to scrub your back."

"That sounds like a reasonable wager," Clint said. He was more than a little dumbfounded by the woman's boldness, given their surroundings.

She looked at him with eyes that seemed to be both gray and green.

"I'd consider it an honor to do that for you."

He looked right back at her, feeling his groin begin to ache.

"Why don't you accompany me to my room then, young lady?" he asked, extending his arm.

She nodded and said, "I shall be delighted to do that very thing," and took his arm.

THREE

The bronze tub was long enough for Clint to stretch out completely.

After eight buckets of hot water and a complete soaping, Clint felt as clean as a newborn infant.

Kate O'Hara wielded the scrub brush with erotic grace.

"You've a well-muscled body," she said.

"Thank you."

He glanced around the room. Flocked wallpaper and heavy, mahogany furniture lent the place a palatial air.

"Of course," she said, "Jim West did say that you were a lady pleaser."

"Jim West?"

She laughed and the sound played along his spine, giving him the chills.

"Oh, sure, and I suppose you're used to mysterious ladies inviting themselves up to your room after just a glance?"

Clint didn't want to sound immodest, but it had happened to him on more than one occasion.

"I should have known," he said, "that sooner or later they'd get around to hiring beautiful Secret Service agents."

"Thank you, sir."

"You can't have been with the service long, though. You hardly seem old enough."

Playfully, she said, "And just how old would you have me being in your mind, Mr. Adams?"

"Twenty, at most."

"May the saints shine favors down on you the remainder of your days on earth."

"You're older than that?"

"I should say so. And at a mere twenty-seven years of age I've what they call 'crow's feet.' ''

"You can hardly notice them."

"I thank you for that, Mr. Adams. You're very polite."

"Will you quit calling me 'Mr. Adams'?"

"I suppose I could."

"I mean, I have the feeling we're going to become friends."

One of her small hands slipped into the sudsy water and took hold of his hard shaft.

"Very good friends," she said.

Kate O'Hara's body surprised Clint. She was more

womanly underneath her clothes than her girlish form let on.

Her full breasts with their small pink nipples tasted of her and were as sweet as Clint could recall.

There on the double-sized bed, with the imposing skyline of Denver at dusk filling the northernmost window, Clint brought her to several quick climaxes, keeping his flicking tongue on her until she shook with a frenzy that approached madness.

Then it was her turn.

She treated Clint Adams to the most gentle and the most violent lovemaking he'd ever experienced.

After long minutes of moving her kitten-like tongue over his newly washed body, she mounted him and rode him as if he were a human bronc in need of breaking.

After working him up to a near climax that threatened to blind him for life she then withdrew and began to use her small, deft tongue again.

Clint wondered how much more he would be able to stand.

Finally, her tongue found his cock and began to do all sorts of wondrous and maddening things to it. It darted around the swollen head, up and down the shaft, and then she took him wholly into her mouth with a loud moan.

Just when he could stand no more of it she eased away from him again, rolled over onto her own back and guided him into her.

In the afterglow of the wonderful sex Kate O'Hara brought them back to reality.

"I wish we had more time together, Clint, but I'd better tell you now why Jim West asked you to come here."

Clint put his arms around her and settled back while she explained.

FOUR

Four years earlier a preacher named Gerald Wellfall
had appeared in the city of Denver without fanfare. For
a time the best church he could offer was a storefront
populated mostly by the impoverished. Unlike most
ministers, the Reverend Wellfall seemed to have an
abiding hatred of life's unfortunates, so much so that he
felt no qualms about contacting rich people and
marketing his church's unfortunates as virtual slaves.
They did every kind of work imaginable for fifteen cents
an hour—half of which went to Wellfall. He sold so
many people into this kind of servitude that he soon

grew prosperous and got himself a new, much fancier church.

From what Jim West had been able to piece together, according to Kate O'Hara, it was around this time that the good Reverend first heard of the waters in the mountains, and of how they supposedly healed people of illnesses ranging from gout to cancer.

Wellfall spent a day there, exploring a natural pool inside a large cave, and came away a changed man. He saw a way out of dealing with poor people. Through letters sent across the United States, he began inviting wealthy citizens who suffered from any sort of infirmity to come to Denver and know firsthand the remarkable healing powers of "God's Cleansing Waters."

Not many people came, not at first, but a few came and the waters made them feel better and so more came and within two years Reverend Wellfall had built his castle, constructed stone-by-stone to resemble one north of Glasgow, Scotland, and started to know real power. The rich and powerful sought him out and courted him.

So quickly did he rise to popularity that many U.S. senators felt the need of his endorsement in their re-election campaigns. Newspapers were filled with stories about the wise Reverend. It certainly didn't do a politician any harm to win the man's kind words.

But through an embittered former employee, the Secret Service learned that the Reverend's plans ranged far from religion. Through some sort of affiliation with occult powers, the former employee disclosed, the Reverend planned to take control of certain key people —powerful people in Washington, D.C.

The first such man was Senator Thomas F. Selkirk of Virginia, Senate leader and man thought by many to be the next president of the United States.

Selkirk suffered from painful arthritis. He was presently a guest at Wellfall's castle where he hoped the waters would cure him. From what the ex-employee said, Wellfall had other, more diabolical plans.

James West was in the middle of an investigation involving some very skillful forgeries of American greenbacks and so he'd dispatched Kate O'Hara to meet with the Gunsmith. West hoped that the two of them could find out exactly what was going on at the Reverend's castle before the man could consolidate more power.

"And so that's what we're to do," Kate said. "Stop the Reverend before he can carry out his plan."

"Which is?"

"We're not exactly sure yet, but from what our informant said, the Reverend has made a great study of Jamaican religions."

"Jamaican religions? I don't know a thing about them."

"Have you ever heard the word 'zombies'?"

He shrugged.

"They also refer to them as the living dead."

"That's crazy."

"They're not really dead. They're just under some kind of a spell. And that's what Wellfall has spent his time studying. How you can control the minds of others."

"That sounds almost as crazy as the living dead."

"Are you interested?"

That really wasn't the point. If Jim West wanted his help Clint was willing to give it to him, but it helped if the job interested him.

And, with talk about living dead and mind control, this one did.

He reached for her then and pulled her atop him. Her nipples were hardened little nubs digging into his chest.

"I wish I could control your mind."

"Oh, sir, and just what is it you would have me do?" She reached down and touched her hand to his rising cock. "It certainly wouldn't be anything sinful, would it?"

"Very sinful."

"Oh, sir . . ."

He rolled her gently on her back and they went at each other with a fierceness that made the bedsprings sing.

An hour later, dressed and about to leave the room Kate said, "Jim gave me strict instructions that on your first night here I was to feed you very well and then take you to the Swami."

"The Swami?"

She laughed.

"You sound like I did the first time Jim told me about him."

"You mean, with a crystal ball and everything?"

"Exactly."

"This thing gets more and more intriguing as we go along. Is there a good reason that we're going to meet with this man?"

She laughed again.

"He's the former employee of Wellfall's who contacted the Secret Service."

"I see."

"Actually, you don't sound as if you see at all."

"Well, Swamis, walking dead people, and ministers dealing in mind control are not people I meet every day. Allow me the luxury of a little confusion."

She hugged his arm to her breasts and said, "You need to get out more and meet different kinds of people."

He opened the door and she took a step out into the hallway when suddenly a shot rang out. Clint ducked, but a second before he did he saw a man with a gun crouching behind a huge potted plant.

The next shot gouged a chunk of wood from the door jamb next to his face. Then the man took off down the hall and he drew his gun, intending to give chase when he heard a moan. He fired a shot at the retreating man, then turned to give his attention to Kate O'Hara.

She had slumped to the floor. He knelt next to her and felt for a pulse in her neck. When he had difficulty finding heartbeat the hairs on the back of his head stood up.

Could warm, vivacious, fun-loving Kate O'Hara be dead?

FIVE .

"Please be as quiet as you can."

"Yes, Sister."

"The doctor said you can only stay for a few minutes."

"Yes, Sister."

With that the small nun stepped aside and allowed Clint to enter Kate O'Hara's hospital room.

Four hours had passed since the shooting. Four hours of trying to pace off anxiety outside the room where Kate had been worked on by three different doctors before being moved here.

A midnight moon rode the long, narrow window that spilled fragile silver light across the form beneath the blanket in the room's only bed.

Kate might have been dead, she was so deeply unconscious, but when he looked closely he could see the gentle rise and fall of her breasts.

In the gloom he could make out a chest of drawers, a stand with a ceramic water pitcher, and a partially open closet door. Being more than a bit cautious by nature, Clint walked over and made sure that nobody was lurking inside the closet.

Then he went back and stood over her.

The doctor who had spoken to him after the two bullets were removed said, "I'm afraid I can't give you any kind of definite answer for a few days yet."

"Then she could still die?"

"I hate to say it but if I had to bet, I'd say chances were better for death than life."

So Clint stood above her now and tried to calm himself. Hatred and vengeance seemed out of place in this quiet room, but he couldn't stop himself from wanting justice.

As far as he knew, Kate had not been working on anything else. At least she had not mentioned anything. That made it a good bet that Wellfall was responsible for the shooting.

He looked down at the sickly pale Secret Service agent.

He put out a gentle, careful hand.

She sighed for a moment and he thought she might be stirring but, no, there was only the moonlight and tree branch scraping against the window, and the gentle breathing of the lovely, comatose young woman.

He looked down at her and shook his head, then went

out into the hallway. There was a cold, controlled anger inside of him now, an anger that only bringing the Reverend Wellfall down would satisfy.

A man in a dark overcoat—opened to reveal a worsted three-piece suit—a bowler hat held in both hands and a plump black cigar between generous lips stood in the hall. He was bald and his nose had been broken many times. You did not need a college degree to recognize this man for what he was, a policeman.

The man approached him, shifted the bowler to one hand and held out a hand as hard and thick as a slab of wood.

"Kearny, I'm with the Denver Police Department."

Clint shook the man's hand and introduced himself.

"By God, it is you, then, isn't it?"

Clint frowned.

"The Gunsmith. Wait till I tell me grandkids that I met the Gunsmith."

"I'd rather you tell them what a good job you're going to do protecting that young woman in there from any further harm."

"I'm way ahead of you." He turned and called out, "Hanratty!"

A tall, reed-thin uniformed policeman carrying a Remington shotgun responded to the call by ambling into view from around the corner.

"This is Hanratty," he said, unnecessarily. "Believe me, he may look like a farm boy but he isn't. Anybody tried to get in there, Hanratty will blow his balls off, believe me."

Hanratty grinned, revealing bad teeth and a slightly psychotic gleam in his eyes.

Kearny said, "Let's go get a cup of coffee somewhere and talk."

Clint knew what the policeman wanted and wished he could give it to him.

Because he had been summoned here by James West, and that West represented the Secret Service, and that the Secret Service figured higher in the scheme of things than the local police, Clint knew he couldn't divulge anything to Kearny—at least, not without somebody's okay, and right now Clint didn't know anyone he could get that from.

They sat in the dining room of a hotel across the street from the hospital.

"Why would anyone want to kill her?"

Clint was ready with his answer.

"They didn't."

"I beg your pardon?"

"It wasn't her they wanted."

"You, you mean?"

"Right, they wanted me."

"Because of your reputation, right?"

Clint could see that there was a good chance his story would be believed.

"It happens all the time. Somebody has a few drinks and decides to make a reputation for himself."

Kearny studied Clint for a while, then shook his head in admiration.

"I knew you were good with a gun, Adams, but I didn't know you were this good with a lie."

"A lie?"

"You bet, a lie. This is all horseshit and you know it. Somebody wanted the girl dead and they shot her. They didn't want you or else they wouldn't have missed you from that range. Now I'd like you to tell me who the girl is and why she was shot."

"I don't know. I mean, if they weren't after me, I

can't imagine why they'd be after her. And besides, we had just met in the hotel lobby, tonight. All I know about Kate O'Hara is her name.''

"There you go again."

"It's the truth."

"My behind."

"Would you like some more coffee?"

"Don't change the subject—but yes, I would."

Clint poured them each another cup from the pot, like the perfect host, even though the coffee was on Kearny.

"Are you going to let him get away with it?"

"Who?"

"The killer?"

"She's not dead, yet."

Kearny ignored that.

"I've heard you're a man who is loyal to his friends. It strikes me that after you leave here you'll start looking for the man who did this."

Clint shrugged.

"Let me give you fair warning, my friend. You try any of that horseshit in Denver and you'll find yourself behind bars—or worse." Kearny leaned in, lowering his voice. "This is a civilized town. We've got electric lights and trolley cars and every whore within the city limits has to be checked for disease twice a month by a real medical doctor."

"Sounds like Denver's changed a lot since the last time I was here."

"And I know about that, too. There were a lot of murders the last time you were here, and I'm not saying you were the cause, but I don't want to see that happen again."

"I'll keep all of that in mind, Mr. Kearny."

"It's Lieutenant."

"Lieutenant."

"So you're not going to cooperate with my investigation?"

"I'd like to, Lieutenant, I just don't know any more than I've told you."

"I'm sorry to hear that," Kearny said, standing. He put his topcoat back on and then dug his hands deep into the pockets. "If I have anything to say about it, Adams, your stay in Denver is not going to be a very pleasant one."

"I'm sorry—" he started to say, but Kearny had dismissed him and was turning to leave. "By the way, how is Lieutenant Gorman doing?"

Gorman was the policeman that Clint *had* cooperated with the last time he was in Denver, over a year ago.

"Gorman? He's retired—permanently."

"You mean—"

"He was shot by a suspect a few months ago. I was promoted to take his place."

"I see."

"So you see, you've got no friends to intercede for you, Adams, if I decide to play it by the book. Good night."

SIX

Twenty minutes after leaving the company of the dour policeman, Clint had asked enough questions of Windsor Hotel employees to find "Swami" Jack.

The Denver night roared with wind and depravity, at least in the neighborhood that Clint now found himself in. Somehow he didn't think that Kearny's new rule about whores being checked by doctors was being followed here. The women who had approached him on the street didn't look as if they would pass any medical tests.

The lights of taverns were the only lights along this

narrow board sidewalk. Occasionally Clint had to walk wide of some unfortunate sleeping drunk. The odors of piss and vomit and cheap perfume imposed themselves on the wind as he made his way through the darkness. The moon had fled behind some clouds.

Finally he came to a three-story place made out of crude pine. The word "Lodging" had been chalked on its front door.

Clint went inside. A desk clerk was asleep at the desk over a dime novel, and when Clint woke him the man immediately said, "We're full up."

"I'm looking for somebody."

"Ain't we all?" the man grinned, remarkably alert for someone who had just been awakened. "Personally, I'm lookin' for a blond about five foot—"

Clint clenched his jaw muscles.

"I'm looking for a man—"

"We obviously ain't got the same—"

Clint cut off the man's smart remark by reaching for him, closing his hand on his shirt and pulling him halfway across the desk.

"I'm going to ask you again, and if you interrupt me this time—"

"I won't," the man said, interrupting him. "I swear!"

"I'm looking for Swami Jack."

"Third floor, in the back. Last room."

"Thank you," Clint said, releasing the man.

If there was a hell, Clint thought, it would probably look like this. As he ascended the stairs he heard the sounds of nightmares, the personal demons of men whose lives had taken turns bad enough to deposit them here. Some cried, some cackled, some called out for their mothers and fathers. Intermingled were the sounds of vomiting and phlegm-hacking, and even an obscene parody of sexual gratification as a woman cried out in feigned passion.

When Clint reached the third floor, he saw that he would have no trouble finding the Swami's place.

Straight ahead of him, at the end of the hall, was a door with several garish astrological symbols and the head of a devil. A kerosene lamp flickered light on the devil's head, giving the thing an eerie life. Clint reached the door and raised his hand to knock but realized the door was slightly ajar. He eased the door open the rest of the way and went inside.

At that moment the Reverend Gerald Wellfall was examining the naked form of a beautiful young woman.

She lay on a raised slab of marble much like an altar. Behind the slab glowed a greenish light that tinted the features of a tall, thin black man dressed in the colorful attire of a Jamaican witch doctor. With stripes of paint across his nose, eyelids and chin, the man's face looked like a mask.

"Rise and do the bidding of your master," Lee Powell, the black man, said, addressing the young woman on the altar.

Reverend Wellfall spoke. His voice was even more like rolling thunder than usual in the cavernous room, and he sounded impatient.

"It isn't working."

"Perhaps the potion I gave her—"

"The potion be damned!" Wellfall said loudly. "You know what must happen within the next few days. If you cannot even get a young girl to be susceptible to your techniques how are we going to get a United States Senator to fall prey to them?"

Lee Powell turned back to the black girl.

"Rise and do the bidding of your Master!"

For the moment the Reverend contented himself with the sight of the girl's body, lush as it was. Large breasts with silver dollar-sized pink nipples; a luxurious thatch of pubic hair that revealed a hint of lips that would taste as sweet as summer berries.

In the midst of his erotic fantasies, the Reverend Wellfall noticed something else.

"Look!"

In the greenish glow the Reverend could see—unmistakably—the young woman's eyes begin to flicker.

"You have brought her back!" the Reverend said, moving closer to the altar for a better look.

Her eyes came fully open and she looked at the Reverend and smiled.

"Are you my master?"

Reverend Wellfall looked at Lee Powell and said, "This is what Jesus did with Lazarus."

Lee Powell just nodded and tried to look solemn, but he could not keep a trace of pride from curving his lips.

In the room where the man known as Swami Jack plied his strange trade, Clint found a hovel that had been made worse by a recent ransacking.

In a corner of the room a chubby man wearing a turban lay on a cot. Clint went over and knelt next to him to see if he were dead or alive. As he did so he found something disturbingly familiar about the man.

Just at the moment he realized who it was the man opened his eyes slightly and peeked at the Gunsmith to see if he were planning him any harm.

"I don't have any money, Sir, if that's what you're looking for at this time of night."

"Get on your feet you silly looking bastard," Clint said, standing up.

"Look here, whoever you are," the plump Swami blustered, "you don't have any right talking to me like that."

"I said, on your feet."

"Wait a minute—" The man had recognized Clint. "Are you—"

"That's right," Clint said. "I'm Clint Adams and you're a poor excuse for a con man named Jack Dolan."

"My God, it is you! Clint Adams!"

With that Dolan struggled to his feet, his turban falling off.

The Gunsmith picked up the fancy headpiece and carried it over to where a kerosene lantern was outlined against a window, and lit the lamp.

With some light in the room the place looked worse than ever. Jack Dolan was doing no better than he ever had.

Clint found a bottle of bad bourbon on a nearby table. He poured each of them a drink and, with no little amusement, invited Dolan to sit down in his own place.

"Still running scams, eh, Jack?"

"Swami Jack, if you please."

"Excuse me."

For all his gray-flecked hair, jowly cheeks and blue altar-boy eyes, Swami Jack Dolan at fifty-four still remained youthful looking. He even managed, at certain times, to effect an odd air of innocence, a trait that Clint Adams had noticed in many con artists. They had to believe their own stories almost as much as their marks did or they wouldn't be able to tell them believably.

Swami Jack Dolan shrugged with a certain amount of sadness.

"I ain't looking for the big one anymore, Clint. I'm just trying to survive. A little piece of work here, a little piece of work there." Then his cheeky Irish face grew curious. "Say, how did you know where to find me?"

Clint smiled.

"You still owe me fifty dollars from Kansas City. I've been tracking you down ever since."

Swami Jack had "borrowed" fifty dollars from Clint, and then had left town.

It took Swami Jack a moment to realize that Clint had been joking. Then he said, "Seriously, how did you know about me being in Denver?"

"A pretty young lady named Kate O'Hara told me."

"Kate—" The Swami looked startled.

Clint indicated the ransacked room.

"I've got a feeling that the same people who visited her visited you."

"Visited her? Is she all right?"

"As a matter of fact, she's far from it."

Clint filled Swami Jack in on the events of the night.

"Those bastards!"

"Who?"

"Reverend Wellfall and his people."

"Tell me about them?"

The Swami wiped tears from his eyes—tears which startled Clint.

"One night one of his ministers—a man named Kirk who's very interested in that occult stuff—came up here to check me out. I staged a seance, and he started to talk too much. He told me all about the Jamaican, a man named Lee Powell."

"That's the Jamaican religious man?"

"Voodoo, they call it. I managed to get myself invited out to Wellfall's to check things out but I didn't find out anything concrete."

"What were you looking for?"

"Something I could use to turn a profit for myself, what else? Some kind of magic, maybe, that would make it easier for me to work my marks." There was no hint of regret in his voice. Swami Jack liked his calling.

"So I got me a job out there and stayed on for a while. All I learned for sure was that there's this Jamaican voodoo man who was raised by white people and he's the Reverend's right-hand man. Something big is going to happen, Clint."

"How did you meet Kate O'Hara?"

"She followed me to Wellfall's one night and convinced me to work for her."

"She convinced you?"

"She's very convincing, and not in the way you think. I liked her."

"I know. Tell me why the Reverend would risk having her killed?"

"Last night Kirk came to visit me again. I figured he might have known that I was some kind of double-agent because during my seance he started talking about a young woman named Kate. Obviously, he was teasing me, seeing how I'd react. I thought Wellfall and Kirk might have been on to both Kate and me—and from what you say, I guess I was right."

"Why would they ransack your room?"

"For one thing, I wasn't here when they came or they might have done more than that. For another, I guess they wanted to see if I had anything on them, something that I might have taken from Wellfall's place."

"Do you?"

"There was nothing to take."

"You like Kate, don't you?"

"You bet. She's like a pretty little Irish lass I might have for a daughter, if I'd married."

"Good, then I'm going to let you help me get the people who shot her."

"That's Wellfall's people. How do I help?"

"You're going to take me to Reverend Wellfall's castle."

"What? They'll kill me."

"They'll only kill you if they know who you are."

Swami Jack looked closely at Clint Adams and shook his head slowly.

"You haven't changed a bit, Clint. You're just as much a con man as I am."

"Let's not get insulting. Are you still as skilled with disguises as you were?"

"What do you think, I'm really this plump? What the hell have you got in mind?"

"Wrong direction."

"Huh?"

"Not hell, Swami Jack. Heaven."

SEVEN

Shortly after dawn a rickety wagon drawn by two spavined horses left Denver and headed east to the mountains.

Aboard were two men of the cloth, the taller, thinner one dressed in a gray suit, black beard and Roman collar, the shorter, thicker one in the red robes of a bishop. He wore a gray beard.

Three dust-eating hours later they drew within sight of a splendid castle whose spires seemed to touch the sky itself.

Clint Adams, his priestly collar scratching his neck,

had the uneasy feeling that he might be dreaming—you didn't expect so magnificent a sight here.

The closer they got, the more impressed the two men became. The castle came complete with towers, turrets, crennelated walls and a drawbridge. Sitting as it did on the edge of a cliff, it seemed virtually impregnable. Atop the battlements strode men in tight-fitting, colorful uniforms. Their rifles glinted in the sunlight.

From the wall above a guard leaned down and called out, "What business do you have here?"

"We've come to pay our respects to Reverend Wellfall," Bishop Swami Jack said. No longer was he plump, but rather thick, like a tree trunk. Clint wasn't quite sure how the man had accomplished this new look, but he'd managed to transform himself into a totally different person—and Clint Adams, as well.

"And who might you be?"

"I am his Excellency, Bishop Raymond Fortescue and this might be Reverend B.J. Hastings."

The guard still did not look convinced—or overly impressed.

"Wait a moment."

The big doors groaned open and two men the size of gorillas came forward. Without asking permission they began looking through the bags of personal belongings the two men had stored in the back of the wagon. A trip to the church mission in Denver, where they'd left more than twenty-five dollars to help the poor, had gotten them many castoffs from the elderly mission priest. The guards now held up rosaries and Bibles, religious paintings and other paraphernalia.

The guards showed all of this to the man up on top. Finally, the man shrugged and said, "Proceed."

The interior of the castle was, if anything, even more

impressive than the exterior.

They were in a huge courtyard where everywhere men and women strode dressed in clean, white robes, attended to by servants of every nationality, from black to brown to yellow, some of whom were scantily clad, very well endowed men and women. Everywhere there was music—Clint heard a fife, a flute, even a timpany drum—as the patrons of Reverend Wellfall's "healing waters" (many of them no doubt wealthy) lounged in erotic scrutiny of each other, or merely lay back studying the blue sky and racing clouds. The whole scene seemed to be out of some medieval carnival.

From here Clint could see that three of the castle's spires accomodated apartments. People were leaning out, watching the activities below. He had no doubt that these apartments were reserved for the very rich and powerful clients of Reverend Wellfall's, and not the "merely" wealthy ones.

"It's something out of a fairy tale," Clint said.

Swami Jack, having been there before, simply nodded in agreement.

"If you will follow me," one of the guards said. "Someone will see to your horses and wagon."

The man seemed to spit when he said "horses." Clint and Swami Jack had deliberately picked out the lamest looking animals they could find. They had wanted to appear humble.

And apparently they had succeeded.

Lee Powell happened to be passing a window when the bishop and the prelate were being escorted from their horses into the castle proper.

The tall black man who was Reverend Wellfall's most

trusted assistant and confidant stopped to examine the
two men more closely.

From his earliest days back in Jamaica, to the days
when he had been taken by missionaries to the United
States and educated, Powell had always had a sixth
sense about people—especially those who were pretending to be what they were not.

He couldn't put his doubts into words, but there was
something about the stocky bishop and the taller prelate
that struck him wrong.

Just what it was, he was not yet sure.

But if they were to be guests of the castle, rather than
two men who just stayed for lunch and then passed on,
they would bear watching.

Closely.

EIGHT

"How nice of you to stop by," Reverend Wellfall said, smiling.

This morning, after what had apparently been a very good night's sleep, the famous reverend looked almost as glossy as his photographs in the newspapers back east.

In his time Clint Adams had known a very few men like the Reverend. Pampered in every way imaginable. Which helped explain why, at fifty, the man's pink flesh and trimmed hair and flat waistline gave him the appearance of a thirty year-old.

"We feel that Our Lord summoned us here, Reverend," Swami Jack said. "To help you."

Reverend Wellfall obviously tried to keep the amusement out of his eyes and voice as he said, "To help me?"

The Bishop nodded.

"Perhaps you had best explain, Father," the Bishop said to Father Clint.

Thanks a heap, Clint thought. The way they had rehearsed it, this part of the routine was supposed to be the Bishop's. Why had he changed it?

For a moment Clint allowed his eyes to fall on a bar of sunlight that lit up the Reverend's huge office. The whole place was booklined and trimmed in mahogany and fine leather.

"Your waters," Clint began, without a whole lot of confidence. Swami Jack was the con man—and Wellfall the ultimate con man. Clint was simply not comfortable in the part.

"What about my waters?"

"There are millions who need them."

A flicker of displeasure flitted across the Reverend's eyes.

"Yes?"

"Well, we believe the Bishop and I have figured out a way to bring millions some of your miracle waters, and to bring you enormous profits at the same time." Clint cleared his throat and added, "All in the name of Our Lord, of course."

"Of course."

"So we wondered if you would be interested in hearing us out."

Reverend Wellfall made a very big production of taking his pocket watch from his vest and looking at it carefully.

"This happens to be a very busy day for me."

"Millions and millions of people," Bishop Swami Jack Dolan said slowly.

"Millions and millions of dollars," Clint chimed in.

"For the Lord's work, of course," Reverend Wellfall said.

"Who else?" the Bishop said.

The Reverend splayed his hands and looked briefly to the ceiling, as if the Lord Himself were sitting there giving the Reverend a hint or two about what to do next.

"Well," the Reverend said.

"Millions," Bishop Swami Jack Dolan said, again.

"Well," Reverend Wellfall said, "well, all right."

Lee Powell knew the moment he opened the door to the private inner sanctum that something had gone terribly wrong.

The smell told him that.

The smell of death.

Daylight never touched this room. Except for the light given off by the candles, it was perpetual night in here.

He rushed to the dais and the naked girl whom last night he had raised from the dead.

Then he looked with disbelief at the terrible fact that lay before him.

The girl was dead.

Stone cold dead.

NINE

"So each label would have my picture on it?" Reverend Wellfall said.

"Each and every label," Father Clint said.

"And each bottle would cost two dollars?"

"Indeed," said Bishop Swami Jack.

"And of the two dollars I—which is to say the Lord—would receive one dollar and a quarter."

"That's correct."

"My God," Reverend Wellfall said, "bottling the sacred miracle waters is something that never crossed my mind before."

"That is obviously why the Lord sent us," the bishop said.

"Think of the hope and help you would bring the masses," Clint said.

"Yes," Reverend Wellfall said, "think of all that mon—uh, hope."

"That's one hell of a lot of hope," Bishop Swami Jack said—and instantly realized that he might have said the wrong thing.

"You will have to forgive His Eminence, Reverend," Clint said, "he sometimes gets overly excited."

But Reverend Wellfall had not even heard Swami Jack's swearing.

The Reverend was too busy pacing back and forth in front of the window. He always paced when he was thinking, and he was thinking feverishly now.

About money.

"What would we call it?"

"We already have a name," Clint said.

"Uh, to suggest," Swami Jack hurriedly added.

"What is it?"

"Miracle Treat," Swami Jack said.

For the first time in the past ten minutes of excitement, the Reverend looked skeptical. Anger shone in his eyes.

"Gentlemen, I'm beginning to wonder if this isn't all some elaborate joke."

"Not at all," Swami Jack said, maintaining control of the situation. "We come from a very poor diocese and need to raise money."

"If you would let us help you bottle and package your miracle water, and worry about getting it distributed and sold, we'll make money to continue doing the

Lord's work in our way—and you in yours," Clint explained.

"But why would you call it 'Miracle Treat'? You make it sound like some kind of soda pop."

"Exactly," the Bishop said. "We want the whole family to enjoy it, and that means it's got to sound like something good to drink. We'll take the miracle waters, mix in a little food coloring and sugar with it—"

"You're joking."

"No, I'm not. Think about it. A drink the entire family can enjoy but one that will cure everything from arthritis to—"

The Reverend smiled then.

"Yes, I guess I wasn't thinking clearly, was I? Now I can see what you're talking about. 'Miracle Treat.' Yes, that's very good."

Just then there was a knock on the door.

A leather-clad guard appeared.

"It is time for your blessing in the waters, Your Excellency."

The Reverend offered the other two religious men a small smirk.

"You know how it is with the faithful. They don't feel they're getting their money's worth unless you yourself personally do all the blessings and spend time with them." He nodded to the bishop and the prelate and said, "Of course, you will stay the night. After dinner we can discuss this further. What you propose is very, very interesting. I will have someone see you to your rooms."

"You're very kind," Swami Jack said.

"Not at all. If you will excuse me?"

And with that he was gone.

TEN

Half an hour later Clint had climbed from a tub of water and was drying himself with a towel when there was a knock on the door. Since it had been a manservant who had shown him to the room he simply called out, "Come in."

The young woman who entered would never be mistaken for a manservant. She was young, with a sweet face and long auburn hair and was incredibly well-endowed—a fact that was amply apparent due to her skimpy, Grecian-like toga.

"Father," she said, her eyes lowered, "I am here for you."

"Uh—" he said, but he stopped when she touched her white gown and it fell to the floor.

Naked she was a vision. Her breasts were very large and firm, with penny brown nipples. Her belly was slightly convex, her thighs a little chunky. She was a solidly built young lady and Clint—even in his guise as a priest—could not help but react to her.

And in his present state it was obvious.

She looked at him and her eyes widened as his cock rose and elongated until it was standing out from his pubic bush, prodding the air.

"Yes," she said, licking her lips and approaching him.

"Listen, Miss—"

But she wouldn't listen. Her eyes were fixed on his erection as if it had exerted some sort of mind control over her. She fell to her knees in front of him and cupped his balls.

"Uh—" he said, jumping. "We can't—"

She cut him off by running her tongue over the head of his cock, while holding it at the base with one hand. He looked down at the top of her head as she opened her mouth and took him inside and began to suck him.

"Jesus—" he said, and reached for her.

He wondered if Swami Jack were going through the same thing now and how he would react.

About twenty minutes after he had sent the girl away there was another knock on his door. He was fully dressed in the white robe that had been laid out for him and opened the door himself.

This time it *was* the manservant.

"I should show you to the waters, Father," the manservant said. He was in his fifties, with the imperious features of a born snob, and the only hint that anything might be imperfect about him was the twitch of his right hand.

Alcohol, Clint thought.

"Is this the time of day?"

"I beg your pardon."

"For the waters."

The manservant pursed his lips.

"The waters never vary in temperature. They remain the same, at fifty-three Fahrenheit, twenty-four hours a day."

"Not exactly like a fishing pond, eh?"

The manservant did not smile at the remark.

"Do you have a name?" Clint asked.

"Yes, sir."

Clint waited. When it was obvious that the man was not going to offer he said, "What is it?"

"Baldridge, sir."

"Will we be stopping at the Bishop's room to collect him?"

"Yes, sir."

"Then I suggest we get started."

When they reached Swami Jack's room Clint said, "Why don't you wait out here, Baldridge, and I'll see if His Eminence needs any assistance?"

"As you wish, sir."

Clint entered the room without knocking and found Swami Jack putting on his robe.

"Did you get a visitor?" Clint asked.

"I sure did."

"It must have been some kind of test. What happened?"

"What do you mean, what happened? This incredible girl with red hair and huge breasts came in, lifted my bishop's robes and swallowed my cock."

"You didn't let her—I mean, you didn't really—"

But the look on Swami Jack's face was enough to answer Clint's question.

"Didn't you?" Swami Jack asked.

"I sent her away," Clint said. It was true. He had reached for the woman, lifted her to her feet, scolded her gently about "sinning," and then sent her away —with great regrets.

"I guess I wasn't as true to my vows as you were, Father. She sucked me until I came, and I thought the top of my head was going to come off."

"Jack, damnity—"

"Don't worry," Swami Jack said, "I scolded her and told her she was a sinner and that she had made me sin, too."

"We could be dead—"

"Not necessarily," Jack said. "After all, Clint, men of God *are* just men. You resisted temptation and I didn't. If it comes up I'll look properly ashamed, but I'm also older than you. They'll assume that I've gone without longer than you have."

"I hope so."

"Besides," Jack said, "it isn't every day *I* get an offer like that, you know."

"Oh, shut up."

Clint was annoyed that he'd had to resist, and Swami Jack had given in and then managed to explain it away.

"We'd better get going. Baldridge is outside."

"Who?"

"The manservant."

"All right, let's go."

"Wait a minute."

"What?"

"The girl, she didn't get a look at your disguise, did she?"

"She didn't lift my robes high enough to see the padding I'm using—she only lifted it high enough to see what I hadn't disguised at all."

Clint frowned and said, "Let's go—and get that silly grin off your face!"

ELEVEN

The cave was vast enough to march an army through. The place was a seemingly endless Chinese box of chambers and broad corridors, walled on either side of limestone formations that were both beautiful and repellent. Small tracks had been laid so that guests could be transported deep into the cave in carts big enough to contain four people.

Clint and Swami Jack rode with a beautiful young woman who'd been introduced as Gretchen Oliver, and an angry-looking man named Ben Tolliver.

Clint and Jack took turns letting their eyes feast on Gretchen.

From behind Clint could feel the eyes of the manservant, Baldridge, on him, and wondered if he was noticing the looks he and Jack were giving the young woman.

Remembering that Kate O'Hara lay gravely ill, perhaps dying, in a hospital bed, Clint got into character once again. He looked straight ahead and ignored the beautiful, bountiful Gretchen.

Nothing could have prepared him for the scene he saw next.

Vines and flowers of every sort imaginable were strung along cave walls. Waiters in formal attire walked between large banquet tables filled with food. A six piece string quartet played sweet popular tunes of the day. More than a hundred people, old, young, attractive, ugly, healthy and crippled sat sipping wine at the tables, or diving into the waters, or sitting near the waters and allowing the bubbling waves to rush up to meet them. There was even a dance floor where couples moved around as if they were at a gala.

The tracks on which they rode ended on a ledge that overlooked the restaurant.

Clint and the others left the cart and went below to join the festivities.

Clint had been wondering if Gretchen Oliver and Tolliver were together. They proved not to be. Sourly, Tolliver went off by himself.

Gretchen looked around, her strawberry colored hair and pert nose as ravishing as ever.

"Would you care to join us?" Clint asked her.

She looked around the crowded, noisy place. She seemed to be as new to all this as they were.

"What a grand idea."

She had a fancy way of speaking which Clint found both irritating and cute.

Swami Jack shot Clint a glance and together the three of them found a table.

As they were being seated, Gretchen nodded to a white-haired man who, in his toga-like robe, resembled a Roman senator. Gretchen, on the other hand, was wearing the costume that all the attractive young women seemed to be wearing—a toga style short gown that barely reached her knees—which made her look like a Roman slave.

"Do you know who he is?" she whispered.

Clint shook his head.

"Senator Thomas P. Selkirk."

"What's he doing here?"

Gretchen shrugged her lovely shoulders and said, "I'm not sure."

His next question should have been why she was so interested in the Senator's presence, but he knew better than to ask. For all he knew he might embarrass the young woman—perhaps she'd visited Selkirk's room the way two young women had visited him and Swami Jack not long ago. Then again, perhaps not, for she was sitting with them as a guest, and not acting as a waitress, as some of the others were doing.

Clint wondered what she was doing there.

A waiter came over and asked for their order.

Gretchen laughed.

"I'd say roast pig," she said, pointing to the huge pig on Selkirk's table. "Would that be all right with you two gentlemen?"

Clint and Jack exchanged glances, again. Clint was

used to beef jerky and trail stew while Jack was used to whatever he could find. Roast pig sounded wonderful to them.

"That's fine," Clint said.

"Very good," the waiter said.

When Gretchen turned back to him Clint's eyes were fixed steadily on her breasts, the large nipples of which poked at the thin white material of her gown. He hoped that his uncontrollable erection was not poking at the material of *his* gown.

She smiled and her eyes found his.

"So," she said, obviously amused by his studied glance, "I understand you're a priest?"

"You told me it would work, this time," the Reverend Gerald Wellfall said as he paced around the dais where the dead girl lay.

"Something went wrong," Lee Powell said. He was nervous, and when that happened he lapsed back into the Jamaican accent of his youth.

"Oh, that's very helpful, very helpful. 'Something went wrong'," Wellfall mimicked.

"We will get another girl."

"And just where do you suggest we do that. You're not taking any of the girls around here, that's too—"

"I know of one."

"Who?"

"The one named Kate O'Hara."

Reverend Wellfall's face lost some of its anger. That was the girl they suspected of being a Secret Service agent.

"She's still in the hospital, isn't she?"

"Yes."

"But how could we get her here?"

THE DEADLY HEALER 49

Lee Powell drew himself up, keeping his black face inscrutable, and said in perfect English, "I will summon her here."

"Do you realize what will happen if you get caught?"

"I will not be caught."

Wellfall looked over at the dead girl again. Her flesh had started to turn blue. She had been such a lovely one. He'd had fantasies about having sex with her when she was brought back to life, to see what kind of an experience it would be.

Now it would not happen.

Not with this woman, anyway.

"All right," he said, thinking of the beautiful Kate O'Hara, "get her, then."

The black man, attired in a three piece suit dark as the ebony sky, bowed and vanished from the room as quickly and silently as a shadow, leaving Wellfall standing next to the dais and the dead woman in the eerie light of the cavern.

Wellfall shook his head.

Senator Selkirk was scheduled to leave them the day after tomorrow. That did not give them much time to carry out their plan.

With Selkirk in their control—*his* control—they would then seize the President himself.

Before long, the good Reverend Wellfall would be more powerful than any mere elected official had ever been.

TWELVE

Half an hour later, when Gretchen excused herself, Swami Jack leaned over and said to Clint, "What a body!"

"Shh, not so loud," Clint said, "but you're right. I think she might be getting suspicious of us, though."

"Why's that?"

"We're supposed to be men of the cloth, Jack," Clint said, "and you keep undressing the girl with your eyes—not that she's all that dressed in the first place."

"What about you?" Jack asked. "I suppose that's

your gun?'' He was looking directly at Clint's crotch.

Clint shifted his legs in an attempt to hide the painful and insistent erection. No, it wasn't his gun, and that reminded him of how naked he felt without the weapon, which was hidden among his belongings on the wagon.

Had the wagon been searched? If so, did they wonder what a priest was doing with a gun?

"I wonder what Wellfall thinks of us?" he asked, changing the subject.

"I think he buys it. Did you see the greedy gleam in his eye?"

"He's got to be a little leery, though. If he wasn't he'd be stupid, and he's not stupid."

"I agree."

"I wonder where this Lee Powell is that Kate mentioned? I want to get a look at him."

Gretchen came back, suspending conversation, and their dinner was served.

The pig had an apple in his mouth.

"It's a good thing he's dead," she commented.

"Why?" Clint asked.

"Because he looks so ridiculous that I think if he were alive he'd die from embarrassment."

Clint laughed genuinely and said, "I guess you're right."

He was aware of the young woman's sense of humor and brains as well as her fabulous body. The conversation they had been having was intelligent—maybe too intelligent.

What was she doing here?

The waiter had just asked them for their choice of dessert when the screaming started.

Clint, accustomed to trouble, tensed at the sound of the screams and rose from his seat at the table to try and track their source. He went to the edge of the shelf they were on and looked down towards the waters.

At first glance everything seemed to be fine. People of various ages lounged in the water. Some were playful, others almost prayerful in their movements. The blue water bubbled up from a natural well below. Clint hoped that they were enjoying it. They had paid handsomely for the privilege of being there.

Toward the other side of the cave, where the limestone ceiling pinched to form a narrow passageway into another part of the cave, the water swelled into deep waves.

It was here that the man known as Ben Tolliver, who had been a passenger in the cart with Clint, Swami Jack and Gretchen, was apparently drowning.

He bobbed up and down, waving frantically and yelling for help.

Nearby, a couple of women continued to scream.

Clint reacted instinctively. He ripped off his robe, clad now only in his underwear, and dove straight down into the water.

Fortunately, he was a good swimmer. He reached the floundering man with no problem.

The man was half crazy with fear, which made his rescue more difficult than it needed to be.

Several times Clint caught an elbow in his mouth or head, enough so that at one point the flailing Tolliver cut Clint's lower lip.

"Just calm down," Clint shouted, trying to get his arms around Tolliver's shoulders so he could guide him back safely to shore.

In all the excitement Clint had forgotten one thing. He was wearing a beard which was held on only with theatrical glue. Jack had guaranteed that the beard would stay on even when wet, but at this point it was soaked and it slipped just long enough for Tolliver to get a good look at his rescuer.

The man's face, in spite of the fear he was feeling, betrayed the shock of recognition. Clint grabbed him harshly with one hand while jamming the beard back into place with the other, and began to steer the man back to safety.

The onlookers made a big thing out of the rescue, much more so than Clint wanted.

Tolliver lay on a shelf of rock, getting his breath and regaining his composure. Obviously he was a strong and virile man and he saw something embarrassing about having to be rescued like that.

His gaze seemed to contain many different things for Clint—gratitude, resentment, curiosity—and a touch of triumph, as if he had something on Clint.

Which, indeed, he had.

He knew who Clint really was.

For now, however, there was no time for Clint to worry about that.

Gretchen was there, throwing a robe over his chilled body and pressing her firm breasts against him.

Playing a priest under these circumstances was no easy task. For the sake of distraction he walked over to where Tolliver was now sitting up.

"Are you all right?"

"Yes."

There was no hint of friendliness or gratitude in the man's tone.

"Just got out a little too far, huh?"

"If you're looking for some kind of a reward, you've come to the wrong place."

"No reward, friend. I just wanted to check and see how you were doing."

"Well, you've seen, so why don't you get the hell away from me?"

"What an ingrate you are," Gretchen said. "This man saved your life."

Tolliver stood up, glared at them and then stalked off.

"I think you hurt his pride, Father," Bishop Swami Jack said from behind Clint.

"Apparently."

"He's still an ingrate," Gretchen said. "Now come on, Father, I'll walk you back to your room."

"That's very kind of you, Gretchen, but I'm sure I can manage."

"Nonsense," she said, "I want to make sure you get there safely and get some rest." Her eyes caught his and she added, "I intend to see to it personally that you get warmed up."

Glancing at her body Clint couldn't help but wish they had met under very different circumstances.

THIRTEEN

Sometimes in his dreams Lee Powell relived all of his many previous lives. Curiously, in each former incarnation, no matter who or what else he had been, Lee Powell had always known the powers of a *hungan*, a voodoo priest.

Standing outside the hospital on the outskirts of Denver, he now invoked those powers once again.

Cupped in his hand was a tiny, tinkling bell with which he could summon those who had lost consciousness.

On the gathering night air, the bell sounded faintly, and the sound travelled.

Then, gradually, a smile parted the tall black man's lips and he looked up at the second floor window, behind which his prey reclined.

She was seven years old again back in Wisconsin, watching her mother make butter. Then she was a sixteen-year-old dancing to the tune of a fiddle in the arms of handsome Johnny McGrath. Next, she was twenty-five and being sworn in as a Special Agent assigned to James West—

Kate O'Hara came out of her deep sleep soaked with sweat and in terrible pain from the bullet wound high up in her chest. A little higher and to the right and it would have simply been a shoulder wound. A little lower and to the left, and the bullet would have pierced her heart.

I am He for whom you have waited.

She seemed trapped between waking and sleeping and could not tell if the voice she was hearing was real or simply part of a dream.

I am He.

Come.

She pushed the covers back with surprising strength and walked over to the window. Down there, black as the early night itself, she could see a man holding a tiny bell which seemed to glow as if infused with hellfire.

Bell and man alike summoned her.

I am He for whom you have waited.

It was then that Kate realized how the man was communicating with her.

Mind to mind.

Apparently he found words unnecessary.

Come.

But she knew better.

Knew that she should not be drawn into this man's strange games.

She went back to bed and crawled under the covers, attempting to close her ears, her *mind*.

She began to hum, and then pray, seeking some way to drown out the incessant summoning that was going on inside her head.

Come.

But she would not.

She would resist no matter what.

Or at least, she hoped she would.

Lee Powell put the bell away after a time. That had not worked. Sometimes his powers were stronger than others. This woman had found it inside herself to resist him.

From the ground next to him he picked up a large wicker basket. It was very heavy. Inside was coiled a rattlesnake, fat with malice.

Lee Powell reached down and seized the snake behind its head. Their eyes met, snake and man, and then a curious light seemed to come from the center of the reptile's gaze.

You will do my bidding, the *hungan* told the reptile.

And the reptile, whose ancestors had known many such men down through the corridors of time, had no will to resist.

The rattler found a basement window open. From the coal bin it slithered to the floor where patients whose recovery was well along were being visited by families and friends.

Several times it seemed that the snake would be seen,

but it eluded being sighted as if it knew the price the
hungan would extract for failure. It went up the small
dumb waiter in the rear of the hospital to the second
floor.

There, where the seriously ill could be found, it had
little trouble. The nurses were taking their dinner break
and the shadows were sufficient to make sighting
unlikely.

When it found Kate O'Hara's room, the strange light
at the center of its eyes showed once again.

The snake entered the room.

Kate lay in her bed, thinking that she had outsmarted
the black man watching the hospital. Obviously, he was
connected with Reverend Wellfall, and was quite
possibly Lee Powell, himself.

The Reverend still wanted to pay her back for the information she had gathered, but—if only temporarily
—she had beaten back another attempt on her life.

If only she could get in touch with Clint, or West.

Her eyes became very heavy at that point, and she
slept.

Somewhere between sleeping and waking she felt the
presence on the bed.

She reached down and felt the scaley shaft of the rattlesnake next to her and began to scream. Before any
sound could come from her throat, though, the snake
reared and bit her.

From two glands, one in each cheek and carrying
along a duct to its two, needle-like teeth, the rattlesnake
filled Kate O'Hara with poison.

But this was not its usual venom, for now the rattler
was acting as the proxy of Lee Powell.

Instead of dying, the beautiful young woman fell into a deep coma, one that could be penetrated by only one man.

Lee Powell.

This time when he summoned her, she came.

FOURTEEN

While Kate O'Hara was being summoned from her hospital room, Clint Adams lay on his bed in his sumptuous suite in Reverend Wellfall's castle, thinking fondly of how Gretchen Oliver had walked him back from the cavern of the waters and made such a fuss over him.

·When they had reached his room she started to remove his robe, pressing her breasts against him as she did. He resisted, but she insisted that she be allowed to help. With the robe off, her hands came in contact with his flesh, sending shivers through him.

"See," she said, "you've caught a chill."

He didn't bother pointing out to her that a chill had nothing to do with it.

"You've got to get that wet underwear off."

Was this a test, as the first woman might have been? Was she going to pull off his drawers and swallow his cock? If she did would he be able to restrain himself this time. As young and lovely as the first woman had been, Gretchen was much more fetching.

"I can do that," he said, gently removing her hand from his hip.

"Oh, I'm sorry . . . Father."

There was an inflection in her tone when she called him "Father", and a gleam in her eyes, but she turned her back so he could slip into a dry pair of underwear. His erection swung before him and it was only inches from the woman's back. He was sure that she was aware of the effect she was having on him, and was amused by it. He quickly pulled on the fresh shorts and told her she could turn around. When she did her eyes went right to his crotch.

They found him a clean, dry robe and she helped him into it. To this point she had done everything but reach down and grab him by the penis. As she stood before him, belting his robe, he was able to look down at her full, firm breasts. He had been sorely tempted to give up his guise as Father Hastings and throw her on the bed. He could always plead irresistable temptation had taken hold of him, causing him to sin.

Fortunately, he came to his senses and let her go after she was sure he was all right.

Night filled his window. The sound of soft guitar music from the courtyard below gave the air a melancholy taint.

He did not like lethargy, this sense of drifting. He wanted to get on with the real reason that he and Swami Jack Dolan had come here. He wanted to think about Kate O'Hara, and not about Gretchen Oliver.

As if in response to his thoughts there was a knock on his door. Gretchen, come to dangle herself in front of him like a forbidden apple? After resisting the other young woman's advances, he wasn't sure how long he could stay away from Gretchen.

He called out for whoever it was to enter.

Swami Jack Dolan in full bishop regalia came in. He'd even added a pair of spectacles to the attire for effect. Had Clint not known who he was, he would not have recognized him.

Jack closed the door and, from inside his robes produced a pint of whiskey.

"Where did you get that?" Clint asked.

"One of the girls. I told them I was concerned about your health. After all, you did catch a chill from your swim, didn't you? This will warm you up."

Instead of handing it over, though, Swami Jack tipped it up and knocked back about a fourth of a pint before sitting down on the bed, facing Clint.

"How did you and Gretchen get along?"

"We didn't."

"I admire your strength, to resist two women in such a short span of time—"

"Get off that."

Swami Jack fell silent and took a little nip from the bottle.

"Is there a place in the castle that visitors aren't permitted to see?"

Swami Jack took a moment to think and then said, "Several, actually."

"Where are they?"

"Well, you can't go where his guards bunk down—and you wouldn't want to. You can't go where his 'handmaidens' stay—that's virtually a harem. And you can't go beyond the red doors."

"What's behind the red doors?"

Swami Jack's eyes twinkled as if Clint had just told a joke.

"I don't know, Clint, I've never gone beyond them."

"Very funny, Jack."

"Your Eminence, if you don't mind."

"I don't know many bishops who drink whiskey right out of a pint bottle."

Swami Jack raised the pint and said, "The Church is very enlightened these days."

"Jack, don't you think you better take it easy on that stuff?"

"I intend to," Jack said, and put the bottle back within the folds of his robe.

"Tell me more about the red doors."

"They're in the basement. Just two big red doors that are guarded twenty-four hours a day. Doubly guarded, actually. A guard each at either end of the corridor, then two guards in front of the doors. Each fully armed, of course."

"Of course."

"But I don't know what's in there."

"Have you ever heard any talk?"

"Not really. But one night I did hear sobbing."

"Sobbing?"

"Yes, a woman weeping, I believe."

"If you can't get into the room, how did you hear that?"

Jack grinned and said, "I was in the basement on the

way to take a peek into the harem—there's an observation window right over the pool and sometimes it's left unguarded—when I heard this . . . wailing. It was almost like an animal's." He shuddered, reached for the bottle and then thought better of it. "I've never heard anything like it before."

"After dinner tonight, we're going to check out those red doors."

Swami Jack gaped at him.

"You don't know what you'll be going up against, Clint. There are guards outside, there may well be guards inside, too. To be frank, I don't know how much good I'll be to you in a real fight."

Clint laughed and said, "You've got to have more faith in yourself, your Eminence."

"You're really going to do this?"

"I am."

Swami Jack did not look happy.

"Listen, Jack, all you have to do is show me where the doors are. I can take it from there. Nobody expects you to risk your life."

"Except maybe that little girl in the hospital," Jack said, thinking of Kate O'Hara.

"Kate wouldn't want you to—"

"No, no," Jack said, haltingly, "if you're going in I'm going with you. We're in this together," he said, then took out the pint bottle and added, "God help us."

· **FIFTEEN**

Senator Thomas P. Selkirk stared frankly at the young woman who had been dispatched to help him dress for dinner tonight.

Despite the pain in his right leg from his arthritis—which had been the reason he'd ostensibly come to Reverend Wellfall's estate in the first place—Selkirk felt unbridled lust for the young woman. In fact, he'd been feeling that way ever since his arrival. Up til now he had not tried to do anything about it.

With his patrician profile he considered himself not unattractive, even to a woman much younger than his own sixty years.

He watched in rapt attention as, bending over to lay out his shorts on the bed, one of her full breasts fell from her loose fitting robe.

His resolve finally broke.

He crossed to her quickly, mouth dry, and cupped his hand over her breast, pressing his groin into her hip.

Her quick reaction startled him. She turned into his arms, slid her hand behind his neck and brought their faces together. Her tongue found his and ignited a fire in the older man.

He could not recall having had an erection this hard in twenty years! His wife had never caused him to become this excited, even when they *were* sharing a bed.

He eased her back onto the bed, his hand parting her legs, his fingers finding her wet, hot crease, his mouth avid on her breasts. She moved one hand between them and began kneading him through his robe. He almost came right there and then!

Abruptly, her hand left him and she said, "Please," pushing him away gently. "I have much to do in preparation for dinner. But later tonight . . ."

"My God, woman, don't tease me."

She leaned towards him, her lovely blue eyes candid. She had an angel's face, long dark hair and smooth skin, the smoothest he'd ever encountered. He could still feel her nipple in his mouth, the warmth between her legs, her hand on his cock . . .

"I want you as much as you want me, Senator. You are the most handsome man in the castle, but it must be later. When we have more time." She kissed him gently on the lips. "The waiting will make it better. You will see."

The Senator was dazzled by the young woman.

"What is your name?"

"Darla."

"It must be tonight, Darla. I will not be denied."

"I know, and it will be."

"Promise."

"I promise."

He grabbed her again, filled his hand with one of her sumptuous breasts, his breath coming shortly.

"Before I go then," she relented, "just to show you I am sincere."

She went to her knees before him, opened his robe and filled her mouth with him.

Senator Selkirk closed his eyes, gripped her head, and moaned. Almost immediately he began to ejaculate into her mouth and as marvelous as it felt, he knew that tonight would be even better.

SIXTEEN

Dinner was formal.

Clint had never worn a tuxedo before and was sure, once he'd stuffed himself into the thing, that he would never wear one again.

A prelate as simple as the good Father Hastings might have to bow to style and wear a tuxedo, but not a bishop.

Swami Jack Dolan was resplendent as usual in his red bishop's robes.

Several entertainment acts appeared on the dais at the head of the great dining hall. There were clowns, jugglers, a barbershop quartet and now a string quartet.

Clint was having a steak smothered in butter, onions and mushrooms while Swami Jack was eating his way through a stack of pork chops. He'd ordered them as if he'd been ordering flapjacks in a drover's restaurant. The prissy waiter had looked offended.

"Maybe you should have ordered a few more," Clint suggested. "You might get hungry in the middle of the night."

"If I do I'll pull the cord and have one of these lovely girls bring me a snack. Besides, I don't know about you but I'll never eat this good again and I want to make the most of it."

"I'm thinking about those red doors."

Swami Jack made a face and said, "I'm trying to enjoy my meal, that's why I'm *not* thinking about the red doors, if you don't mind."

At that point Gretchen appeared, looking ravishing in a shoulderless green gown. Clint smiled and she returned it twice over.

"Good evening, Father, Your Eminence," she said, greeting them each in turn.

"Good evening, Gretchen," Clint said.

The Bishop said something that was rendered unintelligible by the volume of pork chops he had in his mouth.

"Do you mind if I join you?" she asked.

"I don't, but he might."

Gretchen followed Clint's gaze to Ben Tolliver. The surly man was glaring at them from across the room.

"I get the distinct impression that he would like you to dine with him."

Gretchen shuddered and said, "He disgusts me."

Clint wondered if the man had been so angry earlier

because Gretchen had rebuked him.

"Sit then, and eat."

She sat and ordered the same thing that "Father Hastings" was having.

For the next ten minutes they sipped wine and chatted amiably. Gretchen told him about herself, how she was a banker's daughter from Wisconsin who had come here to purge herself of a slightly crooked arm, inflicted on her when she had fallen from a cart as a little girl.

"It doesn't look crooked."

"Take my word, it is . . . and it hurts when it rains, too."

"Then you should be glad you don't live in Seattle."

"Does it rain a lot there?"

"Very much like the rain forests in South America."

She looked at Clint with a frank mixture of admiration and envy.

"You've certainly travelled," she said, "for a priest, I mean."

"That's because there are so many poor, poor souls who need my help."

Swami Jack Dolan coughed on his food and Clint swatted him on the back.

"Is he all right?" Gretchen asked.

"The Bishop," Clint said with a smile, "sometimes eats like one of God's lowliest creatures."

Gretchen frowned, not understanding.

"The pig."

At that she laughed, and Swami Jack frowned.

"God loves even his lowliest creations," the Bishop said sagely.

"Gretchen," Clint said, "do you really feel that the Reverend Wellfall can help you?"

"I hope he can," she said, "but I don't know if I *believe* it. Is that terrible?"

"No, it's honest," he said, and it was probably the only honest thing she had told him.

Right from the beginning of her story Clint had felt that something was wrong. She had recited the whole thing—her girlhood, her father and all—as if by rote, like something memorized.

More and more she began to intrigue him, in more ways than one.

Suddenly, a tall black man appeared.

He was at least six foot five. He moved with the grace of a dancer, and the head of his handsome, startling face was entirely shaven.

Clint had read something recently about a scientist in Europe named Mesmer, and his new science. Some called it mesmerism, others called it hypnotism. He had thought of that the other night when he remembered what Kate O'Hara had said about mind control.

Now he imagined that this was what Mesmer must look like. The black man's eyes shone with an inhuman force, a force that would cause some people to look away in fear, and others to be irresistably drawn to.

The man went to the long table in the front of the room where Reverend Wellfall sat. The man whispered something to Wellfall, and then stood up. Wellfall nodded.

The black man left the table and room as abruptly as he had entered.

"Lee Powell," Gretchen said, noticing Clint's interest in the man.

Clint knew he had to move quickly.

"Excuse me," he said, rising. Both Gretchen and

Bishop Swami Jack looked up at him curiously.

"I'll be back in a few minutes."

With that Clint left the table and, moments later, the large dining room.

He was betting instinctively that the black man would lead him to the red doors and perhaps show him a way in.

At first he was afraid he'd lost the man. Outside the dining room were three separate passageways. The man had disappeared down one of them. Clint made a choice, and by luck it was the right one.

Down the long, narrow corridor, lit on either side by an occasional torch, the black man glided so smoothly and quickly that it seemed his feet barely touched the floor.

Once the man turned around, looking behind him, as if suddenly aware that someone might be following him. Clint hugged the shadows against the wall, and soon the man turned and continued on again.

Five minutes later, after taking many turns in the corridor that was becoming more and more like a tunnel, the black man walked into a well-lit area and stopped.

Two men wearing Reverend Wellfall's gaudy uniforms leveled rifles at the black man, halting him.

Clint's hunch had proven right, so far! The red doors had to be down the corridor behind the guards.

"The word, please," one of the men said.

"Sacrosanct," Lee Powell said.

The guns were withdrawn.

One of the guards lifted the torch from its holder on the wall and took it to guide the man deeper into the darkness behind them.

Sacrosanct.

Now he had the password, and although the guards

might not recognize him, they would have to respect that.

When he turned from the shadows to return, his robe caught on one of the torch holders and jerked it loose from its mooring.

The torch fell to the ground.

The remaining guard came running, his weapon lowered and ready. Clint flattened himself against the wall less than five yards away, smothered in shadows.

The guard picked up the torch and came walking into the corridor.

Clint felt he had no choice but to attack the man. Soon the man's torch would dissipate the shadows, and he would see who Clint was.

Then, no more than half a yard from him, just out of range of the flickering light, the man stopped.

"Nothing," he said to himself, and went back to his post.

Clint gave a short, devout prayer of thanks, and began to retrace his steps, hoping he would remember all the proper turns.

SEVENTEEN

"The worst that could happen is that we might get killed," Clint said sardonically to Bishop Swami Jack Dolan fifteen minutes later.

Gretchen had once again left the two men alone and was talking to different people around the room.

"I even know the password."

"It's too dangerous."

"All you need to do is distract them, Jack. I'll do the rest."

"But if they figure out that I'm part of the plot against Reverend Wellfall—"

"It's not a plot, Jack, it's a plan to bring the man to justice."

"Those are pretty words, Clint, but if they find out I'll be just as dead."

"All right, then," Clint said, "if you want out just say so. I'll understand. I'll just go and do it by myself."

"How?"

"I don't know how, Jack!"

Clint became aware that Gretchen was watching them from across the room, frowning.

"I'll help you," Swami Jack said.

"Fine. We go at midnight."

A note came to Senator Selkirk's table. He recognized the perfume scent on the envelope. It was from the woman who had helped him dress, the woman who had promised herself to him.

The Senator opened the note with eager, shaking hands.

"You look greatly amused, Senator," said Gardner, the railroad tycoon who enjoyed spending his time with people in power, such as the Senator.

Gardner had muttonchop sideburns, dyed black hair and a belly that made sitting close to the table impossible.

"From the scent of the perfume, I'd say you have an interesting evening ahead of you," Titus Gardner said.

"You flatter me, Titus," Selkirk said. "A man my age—with a woman other than my wife—and a young woman at that?"

Gardner reached out quickly and took the envelope from the Senator's hand. He held it to his nose as one might a flower.

"I said nothing about a *young* woman, Senator. Yes," he said, passing the envelope back and forth beneath his prodigious nose, "quite an evening."

Lee Powell stood in the shadows of the altar as his
two Jamaican assistants, as tall and gaunt of face as he,
laid Kate O'Hara flat on the surface of the stone.

Then Lee Powell stepped up to her and began to recite
his incantations.

His assistants recognized it as the real mother tongue
of their homeland, not the pidgin language that had
been influenced and corrupted by centuries of invaders
and conquerors.

The language of voodoo.

That was the true heart of Jamaica.

The assistants watched as the strange glow behind the
altar became even more vivid.

Watched as Lee Powell reached forward.

Ripped the white hospital gown away from the voluptuous young woman.

She lay naked before the men and the sight of a
woman this lovely cowed them for a time.

Even Lee Powell seemed somewhat intimidated as he
gazed on her perfect, upturned breasts and the thatch of
beautiful, red hair between her legs.

It was then that Lee Powell raised the dagger.

Just above her heart.

His assistants gasped.

Powell began to plunge the dagger downward.

"It's too bad you're a priest," Gretchen said as she
stood before the door to Clint Adams'—Father Hast-
ing's—room. "I know it's naughty of me to say that,
but I can't help it."

She'd had a few drinks too many, from what Clint
could see. Her hair was slightly disheveled, spoiling her

look of urban sophistication, and now every inch of her cried out for a romp in the hay.

Clint gritted his teeth as she leaned against him, breasts pressed to his chest, her hands on his body.

"Sometimes I realize that the pleasures of the flesh present certain attractions."

"Have you ever had a woman?"

"I . . . beg your pardon?"

"I'll bet you have, haven't you? Before you were a priest?"

"Well—"

"And maybe even since?"

"Well—"

"Priests are just men, aren't they?" she asked, one hand straying between his legs. She felt the hard column of flesh there and said, "Yes, I see that they are."

"You are enough to bring the dead to life, Gretchen."

She stared into his eyes then and he realized that she was not so drunk as she appeared.

"That's a sweet thing to say, and not at all what I'd expect from a priest."

"I . . ."

"Are you really a priest?" Her hand closed over him, kneading him through his pants. This contact in the hall, through their clothes, had aroused him even more than the naked young woman in his room earlier that evening.

"Yes."

"Why don't I believe you?"

"It must be the devil in your soul."

"Or the devil in your eyes," she said, licking her lips. "I've seen the way you look at me."

"Gretchen—"

She kissed him then, using her lips and her tongue and her teeth, and he knew he was lost.

"Priest or no," she whispered, "I'm coming inside with you."

"Oh, Hell," Father Clint Adams said.

EIGHTEEN

Just as he was about to reach her heart with the knife, Lee Powell turned the blade aside and flung it into the darkness behind the altar.

He had intended to kill her and bring her back to life, but he knew that his influence over the Reverend Wellfall would soon end if he failed in that again.

Now was the time, he realized, for trickery instead of voodoo.

"You may go now," he told his two totally confused assistants.

When he was alone Powell took from his pocket a

small metal disk that opened like a locket.

Inside it was an orange colored powder. He took a small amount of it between thumb and forefinger and applied it delicately to the base of her slightly flared nostrils. Within a minute she had begun inhaling the orange powder.

A terrible seizure travelled the length of her body.

Lee Powell smiled to himself.

The powder was working.

At ten o'clock the knock came at the door.

Clint Adams, dressed in his street clothes, was seated at the window looking up at the spires of the castle silhouetted against the full moon. Gretchen Oliver—if that was her name—was asleep on the bed, moaning every so often and tossing about. He watched her naked body as the moonlight danced on it and knew he should cover her, but he enjoyed looking at her too much.

It was too early for Swami Jack to be at the door, and so it had to be someone else, perhaps another woman to tempt him.

Too late, he thought, I've already been corrupted.

There was no point in advertising that fact, however, so he answered the door and opened it only enough to allow him to look out into the hall.

It wasn't Swami Jack or a woman, it was a rather fierce looking boy in his teens—farm boy big and farm boy mean—clad in one of the Reverend's official uniforms.

"Yes?" Clint asked, affecting a sleepy look as if he had been awakened.

"The Reverend would like to see you and the Bishop."

"Good," Clint said. "I'll wake the Bishop. Go and

tell the Reverend we will be along shortly.

Surprisingly the boy said, "The Reverend has requested that you come alone."

Instantly, Clint felt that there was something wrong here.

"Wait while I get dressed."

The boy nodded and Clint closed the door.

Gretchen moaned again and moved her long, sleek legs. Not more than fifteen minutes ago Clint had been held captive between those legs, and a most willing captive, at that.

When they had entered his room Gretchen had attacked him with complete abandon, pulling his clothes off and then discarding her own. She had fallen to her knees before him and embraced his huge erection with her hands.

"A very unpriestly condition for you to be in, I think," she said. The moonlight lit the room and allowed him to see the mischievous glint in her eye before she took him in her mouth.

He stood that for as long as he could before raising her up and leading her to the bed. There he took possession of her body, exploring it eagerly with his tongue and hands. Eventually, he lay between her legs, tasting her sweetness with his tongue while she clutched his head and fought to keep from crying out. Finally, as her body was wracked by a massive orgasm, she turned her head into the pillow and screamed.

He mounted her then and entered her eagerly, like a stallion who had been led to the mating shed after a long absence. She wrapped her legs around him and trapped him there as he pounded away at her, cupping her buttocks tightly and relishing the preamble to a shattering climax of his own.

Afterward, as she lay sleepily in the crook of his arm she had said, "No, definitely not a priest," and fallen deeply asleep.

He changed from his trail clothes now to his priestly raiments, donned his collar, and went out into the hall where the uniformed farm boy waited.

Something was definitely wrong.

Lee Powell raised the head of Kate O'Hara and extended his long, tapered fingers to her throat, seeking a pulse.

There was none.

Next he took a small hand mirror and held it just below her nostrils.

Again, nothing. The mirror did not cloud at all.

For all practical purposes, the young woman was dead.

Or so the good Reverend would think when Lee Powell presented the woman to him.

When Clint was within the confines of Reverend Wellfall's study, the Reverend, dressed in a red silk lounging jacket, turned away from the window and hoisted his glass.

"I propose a toast."

"I don't have a drink."

Wellfall pointed and Clint looked at a nearby sideboard, on which stood a glass, apparently filled with some kind of wine. He took three steps and picked it up.

"A toast," Wellfall said, again.

"To what?"

"Two things, actually. One to betraying your partner, the Bishop, and two, to both you and I making a great deal of money."

Clint knew how he was probably expected to reply, and he did not disappoint.

"I am a man of God, Reverend Wellfall," he said, "and not in the habit of betraying my religious superiors."

The Reverend hoisted his drink again.

"Let us drink to a better understanding between men. Specifically, between you and I."

He nodded to the young guard, giving him permission to leave.

"Come and sit down, Father, and let's talk."

Clint obliged the man.

While Clint listened for the next twenty minutes to a plan outlined by the Reverend, the comely young woman known as Gretchen busied herself searching his room.

NINETEEN

"And so," the Reverend Wellfall finished, "as you can see, there is no reason for us to split the profits with your Bishop—or with the Church—when you and I can get the job done by ourselves—and keep the proceeds."

"For God's children."

"That goes without saying."

"If you don't need the Bishop, then why do you need me?" Clint asked.

"Ah, you must be familiar with my reputation, my good friend."

"Familiar enough."

The Reverend returned to his pacing, carrying his wine glass.

"There are some who accuse me of cynicism."

"I know that."

"There are those who accuse me of even worse sins than that—of not caring for anything but money, for instance, while children go hungry throughout the world."

"I've heard that, too."

"So if I were to be the most prominent in this venture, it would look as if I were trying to cash in on my name. There would be those who would try and stop us from succeeding."

"I see."

"But if a humble parish priest such as yourself were to announce that you had struck a deal with the great and cynical Reverend Wellfall to get distribution rights to the miracle waters—well, the masses would be much more eager to accept the word of a simple priest than a lofty minister, wouldn't you say?"

Clint nodded. The Reverend was making so much sense that Clint almost lamented that the deal wasn't for real.

"Then," the Reverend pronounced grandly, "while my name will be carried on the bottle in small letters, it will be your image and name that will appear over mine. That way people will be more apt to treat it kindly."

The Reverend paused in his pacing and said, "More wine, Father?"

Clint raised his glass for a refill.

"Now I'll tell you about the second part of my plan."

Gretchen couldn't find much in the belongings of

"Father Hastings", but after what he had done to her in bed—God, her knees were *still* weak—she was all the more convinced that he was not a priest.

The questions were, what and who was he and what was he doing here?

She sat back on her heels in the middle of the floor, still naked, and closed his worn canvas suitcase. She closed her eyes and thought back to their time in bed. While they were making love she'd had little time to concentrate on anything but the sensations he'd been causing with his hands and mouth and tongue. Now she turned her journalistic mind back to the events and studied them coldly.

It became obvious to her that the beard was a phony, and while they were making love she had unconsciously noticed something that came back to her now.

The scars on his left cheek, one straight one that slanted downward toward the corner of his mouth, and another that crossed it at the top. A man with scars like that should not have been able to grow a beard, yet the beard covered it. Consequently, the beard was not real. Now she tried to picture the face without the beard, and when she had done that she smacked her forehead.

Of course.

Clint Adams.

The Gunsmith.

There had been pictures in the paper from time to time of this living if somewhat reluctant legend, and she had seen enough of them to recognize him—and the scars—once she'd mentally removed the beard.

Quickly, she rose and dressed and moved swiftly to the door. She opened it a crack and when she was sure the corridor was empty she sneaked out and hurried back to her own room.

So this was death, Kate O'Hara thought.

There was darkness and there was pain and there was some kind of uncomfortable constriction that she could not identify yet.

Hell.

That's where she must be.

Images of nuns dressed up as penguins floated through her mind.

In school, the nuns had always chastised her for being too boisterous, too nosy, too mischievous—too flirtatious with boys.

Apparently, they'd been right.

Because look where Kate O'Hara had ended up.

No, it couldn't be. Sex under the front steps of the school with a male lay teacher of thirty when she was but fifteen could not have been enough to land her in Hell.

She let some of the anxiety flow out of her mind and thought back to her last conscious moments.

The man named Clint Adams.

The Gunsmith.

The friend of Jim West's.

Broken, shattered images returned to her. She was opening the door from Clint's hotel room when gunfire suddenly erupted and—

—and she'd been hit.

The searing pain came back to her and took her breath away. Vaguely, memories of the hospital, of a somber doctor, of a scurrying nurse, of being awake but not being awake, of a black man outside her window—

—and a snake.

A snake? Yes, for some reason she had memory of a snake.

In her bed.

And someone summoning her without speaking.

Now there was a noise, as of a door opening in a cavernous room, the sound echoing for a full half a minute.

Footsteps.

She tried to open her eyes, but with no luck.

Kate O'Hara had a terrible thought.

Perhaps she was not dead at all, and this was not Hell.

Perhaps this was a place much, much worse.

"The bank account would be in Chicago under a name only you and I would know," Reverend Wellfall explained, further indicating how thoroughly he had worked this out. "In it we would put the proceeds for you—whatever percentage you deem proper. Do you understand?

"This is all too much for a simple parish priest, I'm afraid."

The Reverend looked as if he were preparing himself to become angry, but he quickly regained control.

"You are not so simple as you would like to seem, my friend."

Clint rose and set down his wine glass. Thus far this evening the good and true Reverend had suggested that he betray his friend and religious superior and rake off much of the proceeds earmarked for the poor. He was quite a man, this Reverend.

"Let me think about this generous offer overnight, Reverend."

"Certainly, certainly. But remember, I am offering you something that no one else ever will, or could."

"I realize that, but I need time to sort out my thoughts."

"I understand," the Reverend said. "Perhaps you need time to pray for divine guidance."

If he had been a real priest Clint would have taken offense at that.

"I don't think that this is the sort of thing you pray over."

"No, of course not," Reverend Wellfall said. "Forgive me for my bad joke. You sleep on my offer and give me your answer in the morning."

"I will," Clint said. "Thank you for the wine. Good night."

"Good night, Father. My guard will take you back to your room."

One minute after Clint closed the door behind him Reverend Wellfall said, "All right. You can come out now."

From behind the thick curtains stepped Lee Powell, looking as imposing and malevolent as always. Wellfall knew that he also looked imposing, but malevolence was something he had never been able to conjure up—nor would he have wished to.

"Well, what was your impression?"

Lee Powell had hidden in the curtains so that he could overhear the conversation the Reverend and he had worked out before hand.

This was a test of the priest, to see if he were who he seemed.

"He is not a priest."

"He may have wavered here, but he passed the test with the girl," Wellfall said.

"The Bishop did not."

"If they're not priests, then who are they?"

"That I am not sure of, yet."

Panic shone in Reverend Wellfall's eyes.

"It is all going to come undone, isn't it?"

Contempt played in Lee Powell's eyes. Five years ago he had been little more than a servant to this man. Now he was virtually the man's master—even though the Reverend did not know this.

"Do as I say and things will work out."

Lee Powell walked to the sideboard, poured the Reverend a glass of wine and handed it to him. It created the illusion that he was serving the other man, when in reality he was lulling him into his place.

"By tomorrow evening the men attempting to pass themselves off as men of God will be no further threat to us whatsoever."

"Why?"

"Because I plan to kill them."

TWENTY

"You'd betray your friend, the Bishop?" Swami Jack Dolan said ruefully when Clint told him what had happened in Reverend Wellfall's study.

"For all that money," Clint said, smiling, "sure I would."

"Just see if I ever make you into a monsignor."

The two men stood at the window of Swami Jack's room. It was eleven-forty p.m. and below, in a moonlit courtyard, was splashed a scene of revelry. Candlelit paper lanterns cast red, green, blue and yellow lights on dozens of partygoers who sat at small tables talking or took to the dance floor. A ten piece orchestra played nearby. The ladies wore gowns almost shocking in their brevity, the men wore tuxedos. A few of the more festive wore eye masks that gave them an air both sophisticated and sinister.

"The good Reverend knows how to treat his guests," Swami Jack said.

"Yes," Clint said, "but then what decent man of God doesn't know how to throw lavish parties?"

"As long as he can afford it."

"Wellfall can," Clint said, "and he's still out for more. That is one greedy man."

Swami Jack grinned shakily and said, "He ain't going to take too kindly to anyone who tries to take away what he's got, is he?"

Clint turned to Jack and said, "Are you ready?"

"I hope you remember what I said."

"About what?"

"About not being of any real help if a fight breaks out, especially if it involves guns."

"Don't worry about that," Clint said. "If there's gunplay, I'll take care of it."

"And how do you intend to do that. Did you bring a gun?"

"You're a con man and you depend on your brain," Clint said. "Did you bring that with you?"

Swami Jack knew what Clint meant. He would no more travel without a gun then a con man would without his brain and his wits.

Clint reached inside his shirt and brought out his little Colt New Line. He had stopped at his room for it.

"That toy?"

"In the right hands, even a toy kills," Clint said—but deep in his heart he agreed with Jack. He would have preferred to have his modified Colt, but that had been too big to hide from any search. The New Line had passed through nicely, without being found. He put it back inside his shirt and buttoned it.

"Do you remember what I want you to do?"

"You're really going to let me do this, aren't you? Knowing I might turn and run at a moment's notice?"

"I don't think you will."

"You're putting your life in my hands."

"I know." Clint decided not to add that he didn't have a whole lot of choice in the matter. There was no one else he could turn to.

Swami Jack rolled his eyes and then assured Clint, "I remember."

Two floors above them the Reverend Matthew Kirk was just concluding his prayers for the night. He believed in remaining on his rugless floor until his knees ached and he could stand it no further. Suffering was good for the soul.

He rose now, whispering the last of his prayers, and went to the window.

Another night in an endless series of revelries—of sin.

At thirty-four, a follower of Reverend Wellfall's for the past five years, Reverend Kirk was by now disenchanted with this place and everything it stood for. He was even more disenchanted with what he'd begun to suspect were Reverend Wellfall's experiments with Satanism. Or rather, Lee Powell's experiments, sanctioned by the Reverend.

Five years ago he would never have expected Reverend Wellfall would end up as he had, but then he had not counted on the black man influencing the Reverend as he had instead of being the other way around.

A few weeks earlier Powell had even dispatched Kirk to Denver where he spent the evening in the company of a man named Swami Jack and a lovely woman named Kate O'Hara—a woman he could not yet get out of his mind. Reverend Kirk was at an age where settling down and having a family appealed to him—and certainly the young woman he had met that night had kept those feelings alive in him.

But when he'd reported the night's events back to Lee Powell and Reverend Wellfall, he had a sense that both the Swami and the girl were in grave trouble—that somehow Powell and Wellfall would bring harm to them.

Reverend Kirk shook his head.

To think that there had actually been a time when he had taken Reverend Wellfall's religion seriously—or that Wellfall himself had taken it seriously. That time was past, however, and Kirk wanted out, to find a church of his own where his life could have dignity and meaning—and maybe find a woman named Kate O'Hara again.

He sighed. He was restless and unable to sleep. This was his fifth night of suffering what he was beginning to think was insomnia.

He decided to do the only thing he could.

Go for a walk through the castle.

Then, half an hour or so later, he could return tired enough to sleep.

Reverend Wellfall splashed water on his face. He wanted to go below to the courtyard and put in an appearance with his guests. There was a particularly sumptuous widow down there whom he hoped to bring back to his apartment tonight. He was beginning to tire of the young women he had at his beck and call. He longed for the company of a more mature, experienced woman like the widow.

The image of Kate O'Hara on Lee Powell's sacrificial altar suddenly invaded his mind—and Wellfall shuddered.

Powell had begun to frighten him.

Tonight the Jamaican was going to experiment on two people—Kate O'Hara and Senator Selkirk.

The experiments terrified Wellfall. He did not know which would be worse, if they were to succeed, or fail. If they failed, then his plans to gradually take control of the Senate and, eventually, the White House, would be dashed. If they succeeded—well, bringing people back from the dead was not natural.

There was a special place in Hell for that kind of blasphemy.

He just hoped that, for both their sakes, the soft spoken Jamaican knew what he was doing.

Because Wellfall didn't know what he was doing, anymore.

As they hastened through the maze of corridors inside the castle, Bishop Swami Jack Dolan said, "I could get killed doing this, you know."

Clint looked at him and grinned.

"So could I, Bishop, so could I."

TWENTY-ONE

The narrowing corridor smelled of kerosene from the burning lanterns. Clint and Swami Jack found shadows to protect them.

Swami Jack hurried along the corridor, trying to keep up with the quicker, taller man. In his hand he carried a mysterious black bottle that Clint had given him after they'd stopped off at his room.

Jack went through all of his familiar reactions to danger. His throat constricted, his stomach clenched, a palsy-like twitch played down the length of his fingers. He wished he could be like Clint Adams. Even if Clint was afraid, he managed to keep his fear under control.

Suddenly, Clint grabbed Jack and pushed him against the wall.

The creak of shoe leather and low whispering could be heard around the nearest turn.

The two men held their breath as three of Wellfall's guards went past the mouth of their corridor.

Swami Jack stained his Bishop's robes with blotches of sweat. He wondered why Clint had insisted he wear them instead of something less conspicuous.

"Thought they might have had us, didn't you?" Clint asked, and Swami Jack could *feel* him grinning in the darkness of the shadows.

Swami Jack nodded.

"So did I."

"Are you going to explain to me your plan for getting into that room?"

"Why, Swami Jack, I figured an old con man like you would have figured it out by now."

They were speaking in whispers.

"Huh?"

"You're going to distract them."

"You told me that," Swami Jack complained, "what you haven't told me is how."

"It's very simple."

"Yeah, I'll bet."

Clint pointed to a torch, and Swami Jack had to squint to see him.

"I don't get it."

"Fire."

"Fire?"

Clint nodded to the black bottle that Swami Jack was holding.

"Kerosene," he explained. "I emptied it from some of the lamps in the corridor outside our rooms."

"What am I going to do with this stuff?"

"Why, you're going to douse yourself with it."

Swami Jack started to protest loudly and Clint pressed his hand over his mouth to quiet him.

There was a wind off the mountains that caused Lieutenant Kearny of the Denver Police to try and bury himself in his wool-lined jacket.

He rode a brown bay across a rocky, moonlit piece of land that slanted uphill towards something out of a fantasy—a castle.

The detective, who had once been a Pinkerton man, had been called from his warm bed to investigate the curious disappearance of a hospital patient—the same Kate O'Hara whose shooting he had investigated earlier.

His reason for heading out to Reverend Wellfall's castle was simple enough—two of the nuns told the detective of seeing a strange, tall black man standing across from the hospital an hour or so before the woman's disappearance was discovered.

Kearny had long had doubts about the whole operation out here at the castle. Strange stories had filtered back to Denver of all kinds of occult events taking place. A practical man, Kearny put little store in the supernatural. He knew, however, that the occult could many times provide a perfect setting for some very human crimes.

He spurred his horse on through the singing, cutting wind to the castle silhouetted against the moon.

Ben Tolliver had not worn his guns since that terrible night in Abilene.

Now he stood in front of the full length mirror in his

room in the castle and contemplated the image of himself as a gunfighter which, in fact, he had been until six months ago when, suddenly, his nerve had given out.

And his reputation had been ruined.

Throughout the three-state area where his name had flourished he had come to stand for cowardice. He had walked away from a fair fight, leaving his opponent to choose between backshooting and letting him go. His opponent had chosen to let him go and live out his terrible fate of a coward.

Tolliver was tired of running, of hearing snickers behind his back. Now he had a plan for reclaiming his pride, and an even larger reputation than he'd once enjoyed.

The "priest" who had saved him from drowning that afternoon was no priest at all. He was a man named Clint Adams, better known as the Gunsmith.

Tolliver didn't know why the Gunsmith was here in the guise of a priest, and he didn't care. The fact that the man was present gave him a perfect chance to redeem himself.

He had bribed a guard dearly to bring him the guns that were taken from him when he first entered the castle. Now he slapped his hands to his guns and drew them in a blur of motion.

The speed was still there.

Was the nerve?

That was something he and the Gunsmith were going to find out together.

Kirk spent another sleepless night.

For some reason his mind was filled with images of snakes that slithered over the forms of helpless young women.

One of the women had a face.

A familiar one.

Kirk jerked upright and realized that he had indeed been sleeping—or else, he'd had a waking dream.

A dream which left him with the definite impression that Kate O'Hara was in grave danger—and was somewhere inside the castle!

TWENTY-TWO

Swami Jack didn't have to fake the screams that came from his mouth once the flames started shooting up the skirts of his bishop's robes.

The plan had gone off exactly as Clint had hoped.

While he circled around to the right side of the guard's station, Swami Jack went left, doused the hem of his robes with the contents of the black bottle and dropped a match on the damp spot to ignite the flames.

And ignite they had.

The two guards, seeing what had happened, came running forward to help the portly religious man who seemed to be devoured by the fires of hell itself.

While the guards were distracted Clint darted from his hiding place and found his way to the red doors at the end of the tunnel.

He slipped inside without being seen.

While no one had ever accused Clint of being a devout man, he had spent some time in churches, including a cathedral or two. He recalled the feeling of awe that the vast churches had inspired in him. He was filled with a different kind of awe now—a sort of vast dread.

Maybe it was the smell of a strange incense, one as rancid as burning flesh. Or maybe it was the spectacle of shrunken heads and devil's masks arrayed along the east wall, their features highlighted by a strange green glow that seemed to emanate from somewhere below the surface of the floor.

Ahead lay an altar, bathed in the same eerie green glow, raised many feet above the floor and almost lost in the haze of incense.

Clint moved carefully across the polished floor toward the altar.

When he reached it he ascended the steps and took a good look at it.

Gutters.

The kind you found in meat slaughtering plants for the blood to run off.

He peered even more closely at the altar.

A few minutes' inspection revealed that the altar was much more than decorative.

Something—animal or human—had been butchered on it.

The closer he got to the gutters, the more intense the stench became, a stench he was more familiar with than he liked to admit.

The stench of human blood.

As soon as Lee Powell arrived and saw that the guards had moved away from their posts, he knew that something had gone terribly wrong.

He went up to them and pointed a dramatic black finger at their empty post.

"What is the meaning of this?"

The guards turned away from Bishop Swami Jack and saw Powell. They knew enough to fear this man.

"But the Bishop—" one man began, defensively.

Powell looked down at the portly man in the bishop's robes.

"What happened to you?"

"My robe caught fire."

"How did it happen?"

"I'm not sure."

Powell's eyes blazed at him.

"Where is your friend, the other priest?"

Swami Jack swallowed, avoided the man's eyes and said, "Probably sleeping at this hour."

"Which makes your presence here all the more interesting," Lee Powell said, leaning over. "Why are you not sleeping?"

"When I have trouble falling asleep I like to go for a late night stroll."

Powell's eyes rose from Bishop Swami Jack and looked off down the corridor that the guards had abandoned. He began to see what had happened.

The man's robes were deliberately set afire to lure the guards from their post.

That meant that the other "priest" had probably slipped into the ceremony room.

Where he could be found.

And killed.

A large smile spread over Powell's face.

"One of you take the Bishop back to his room, to make certain that he is safe." When Powell spoke he was looking at one of the guards, who nodded.

"You needn't trouble yourself," Bishop Swami Jack protested.

"No trouble at all," Lee Powell said. "We do not want you bursting into flames again, do we?"

At that the chosen guard looked dubious about his instructions.

There was no way that Swami Jack could avoid it, so he turned and started down the corridor with the nervous guard two or three steps behind him, just in case.

Finished inspecting the gutters, and convinced that human sacrifices were at least part of the events that took place in this room, Clint began to look more closely at the death masks that adorned the walls.

The fierce images of human death made him uneasy. He was just about to take one of the masks down when he heard one of the heavy red doors behind him creak open.

Quickly, he looked around him for a place to hide.

The prospects were dim.

TWENTY-THREE

When Swami Jack opened the door to his room, he nodded goodnight to the guard who had escorted him there. As he entered he saw the fetching young woman named Gretchen going through his suitcases with the poise and confidence of a professional burglar.

When she heard him she spun around.

While he should have been smart enough to sneak up on her and possibly draw a gun (if he'd had one) it was Gretchen who held the gun.

"Sit down," she said pleasantly. "I want to talk to you."

• • •

Between the back of the dais and the wall there was just enough room for a slender man to hide.

Clint had found the place only moments before the footsteps had come all the way into the room.

From what he could surmise from his awkward hiding place, the visitor was standing in the center of the large room, looking carefully around for any sight of an intruder. He had another odd insight, too. From here the top of the altar seemed curiously loose. There was no time to examine it now, however.

Then the man's voice filled the room with an eerie baritone.

"I know you're in here. It will be only a matter of finding you." A chuckle rippled through the voice. "I even know who you are—or who you pretend to be, shall I say."

Footsteps echoed off the ceiling as the man came forward.

"Undoubtedly, you have inspected the altar and know that we will occasionally sacrifice human beings on it. Such a sacrifice will take place tonight—and you will be the guest."

Obviously Lee Powell was enjoying himself. He appreciated his voice for the dramatic instrument it was. He also appreciated the fact that he had Clint at a distinct disadvantage.

But before he could say more there was a thunderous pounding on the heavy door.

Lee Powell went to it. Clint listened to the exchange with interest.

"What is it?" he demanded irritably.

"The Reverend Wellfall wants you at once!"

"Is something wrong?"

"We have a visitor."

"At this hour?"

"Yes. The policeman from Denver named Kearny."

"Very well. Give me a moment to finish with my work here."

"Yes, sir."

"Tell the Reverend I will be along momentarily."

"Yes, sir."

When the guard had gone, Powell turned back to the room, returning to stand in its center.

"I don't know where you are just yet, but you won't be going anyplace. You see, you may not have had time to check out certain louvered spots along the flooring."

Clint had noticed them but put them down to nothing more than ventilating shafts.

"I had them installed personally," Lee Powell said. "For special friends of mine—like you." His chuckle rumbled through the room once again. "They emit poison gases. I'm afraid nobody's lasted longer than a few minutes. Good evening, my friend."

With that, he strode from the room. In the hallway he bolted and locked the doors. Then he pressed a small button concealed in the woodworking.

The deadly gasses began pouring into the room on the other side of the door.

TWENTY-FOUR

"My name is Gretchen Forbes and I'm a reporter for the *New York Times*," the young lady told Swami Jack Dolan. "I'm here pretending to be a rich socialite seeing if the waters will help my migraines. Actually, I'm investigating Reverend Wellfall."

"So are we."

"You and the Gunsmith?"

"You know who he is, then?"

She smiled.

"His reputation as both a gunfighter and a ladies man is well known."

"Well, I'm worried about him."

"Why?"

Swami Jack explained.

"I wondered what had happened to the hem of your nice red robes," she said. "So he's in this secret room at this very moment?"

"Yes."

For a moment, concern crossed her face. But then she said, "I'm sure if anybody can handle himself, Clint Adams can."

Swami Jack sighed.

"I hope you're right."

Almost instantly, the gases caused Clint to begin bleeding from his nose and mouth.

In Germany, the Kaiser's forces were developing a substance called mustard gas, assuring the world all the while that they were doing so only in the interest of scientific advancement.

Something very much like mustard gas must be at work here, Clint thought, trying to keep his eyes open despite the stinging that brought scalding tears to them.

Maybe Lee Powell had been right after all, the Gunsmith thought, resisting the panic that welled up inside him.

Maybe there *was* no way out of this.

But he'd be damned if he'd give up without trying to prove the strange black man wrong.

By the time another minute had passed the room was virtually filled with the gas.

Clint knew he had a few minutes to live, at best.

Tearing off his shirt and covering his face with the back of it he proceeded to crawl to one of the ducts he remembered seeing. Maybe there was a way to stop the gases from coming into the room.

Finding the duct in the gas filled room was no easy task. Unfortunately, it proved to be a fruitless exercise. The duct was too large, the gas too bilious.

Coughing so hard he could imagine blood in his throat Clint crawled back towards the center of the room.

He had to pause here to fight against the dizziness the gas was beginning to effect in him. Already his skin was becoming irritated and his ears were starting to ring.

He knew he had even less time than he'd hoped.

On his hands and knees he moved back to the dais. His mind, growing more and more desperate, fixed on the top of the altar. He remembered his impression that somehow it had been loose . . .

When he stood up at the dais, the gases so thick now they were like fog on the Barbary Coast, he fell hard against the altar, the dizziness starting to overcome him.

He had little strength left.

He put his hands on the altar top and found that it was actually a thin panel of something like granite. Heavy, but apparently moveable.

At that moment he collapsed to his knees.

His lungs felt as if they were literally tearing apart.

Blood began to spurt from his nose.

He tried to fix his hands on the top of the altar for purchase but it was no use.

He knew now that he had finally met his death, and as he had expected most of his life, it had not come from a bullet.

The Gunsmith was about to die.

Gretchen and Swami Jack hurried along the twisting corridors.

Both showed the effects of their anxiety over the fate of Clint Adams. Gretchen worried her lovely bottom lip with her teeth, and Swami Jack licked his lips, wishing for a drink. He kept looking behind them nervously.

When they reached the guard point they came to a disappointed halt.

"Damn," Swami Jack whispered as they approached.

"You certainly have a vile tongue for a man of the cloth."

But her smirk died as soon as she too saw the guards.

Two of them.

Big, and heavily armed.

"Do you want something?" one of the guards demanded as they approached. These were not the same two guards he had so recently duped.

"No, I guess not," Swami Jack said softly.

Gretchen looked crestfallen. They had charged out of Swami Jack's room without even a plan about what to do when they encountered the guards.

"Then I would advise you to return to your part of the castle," the man said.

Swami Jack saw that they had no choice but to comply.

But where was Clint Adams? And what had happened to him?

TWENTY-FIVE

By now the blood was beginning to trickle from his ears as well as his nose.

Death was at most a minute or two away.

That was when Clint Adams got really angry.

He thought of Lee Powell and Reverend Wellfall and how they'd deceived and betrayed those genuinely interested in religion. He thought of how they were responsible for the shooting of Kate O'Hara, and he thought how blithely they'd been willing to kill him.

Keeping them in mental focus, he found that his rage began to fill his body with strength again. Not all of his strength, of course, but enough for one last ditch effort at coming out of this alive.

He pulled himself up to make one more pass at the altar top. This time he got his shoulder into the act of pushing it, and this time he was rewarded for his effort when the piece moved away from the altar.

Because there was so much thick gas in the room he could not see what lay inside the altar. His only clue was that the thick smoky gas seemed to suddenly be sucked down into it.

He felt something on his face and it took a few moments for his confused mind to identify it.

Fresh air!

What could be down there?

He knew he had no choice but to find out.

Still horribly dizzy, he threw one leg over the opening in the altar and began to feel his way inside.

Within moments he realized what he had done.

Opened the "door"—the top of the altar—to a secret stairway leading . . . where?

He took hold of the ladder on both sides and began to climb down. He had no idea where he was going or what he would find, but it was a hell of a lot better than staying there and waiting to die.

Lieutenant Kearny had been allowed to enter the castle but had been stopped in the courtyard. Waiting, Kearny looked around and thought that the yard looked as if there had been a party going on not long ago.

Several minutes after asking to see the good Reverend Wellfall he was treated to the spectacle of the minister appearing in a very fancy and comic nightshirt.

The Reverend clutched a Bible in his hand and looked completely baffled about why a Denver policeman would be paying him a call at this late hour.

"May I help you, Lieutenant?"

"I hope so. A young woman named Kate O'Hara is missing from the hospital."

Reverend Wellfall clutched his Bible tighter, holding it in both hands.

"I am sorry to hear that, Lieutenant. I do not know the young woman, but I will pray for her safe return."

Kearny decided to go whole hog with this thing and see where it got him.

"I have reason to believe that she may be here."

"Here? What would she be doing here?"

"Frankly, I don't know."

"Then why ask me? I don't know where she is, but she certainly isn't here."

"Your assistant—the black fella named Powell?—he was seen standing across from the hospital just about an hour before she disappeared."

"That's quite impossible. Mr. Powell was here all evening. There are many, many witnesses to that fact, Lieutenant, including a United States Senator. Are you planning to persecute Mr. Powell because of his color?"

Kearny ignored the last question.

"If you're so sure she's not here then I guess you wouldn't mind if I looked around a little?"

"At so late an hour?"

"Policemen are used to such hours."

"Perhaps, but my guests certainly are not."

"I'll try not to upset or wake anyone."

Wellfall compressed his lips for a moment, then said, "Well, all right, then. Step down from your horse and I will have it cared for."

Kearny stepped down and gave up his reins to a huge uniformed guard.

"Come this way," Reverend Wellfall said, and proceeded to lead Kearny into the castle.

When their footsteps had echoed away Lee Powell stepped out from the shadows. In the pale light of the moon Powell's face resembled one of the death masks on the wall in the altar room.

The phony priest had been taken care of, and soon his friend would join him.

This policeman would have to be dealt with.

And so would the Reverend Wellfall.

The events of this night were conspiring to force Lee Powell's long-range plan into action sooner than anticipated.

Perhaps, Clint thought wryly, he had discovered a stepladder to Hell.

At least, that's how far down he seemed to be going. There was a consolation, though. The gases swirled and dipped at the entrance of the shaft, but a breeze of fresh air kept it from following him all the way down.

Abruptly, Clint's foot came off a ladder rung and struck a wooden platform.

He was in a cavern that seemed to have been scooped out of the rock itself, and there were tunnels leading in three different directions. One of them, he felt sure, would probably lead to the waters.

Miracle waters or not, he could sure use a cool dip to clear his senses.

He started to follow one of the tunnels when suddenly he heard a woman's scream.

TWENTY-SIX

"Some tea, perhaps?"

Lt. Kearny shook his head.

"Then maybe something stronger?"

The policeman sighed. It had been a long ride out and he didn't like this man to begin with.

"I have the unmistakable impression that you're trying to stall me." Kearny played with the homburg in his thick hands.

"Not at all, Lieutenant," Reverend Wellfall said.

"Then why don't we leave your study and begin looking around the castle?"

"If you insist."

"I insist."

Reverend Wellfall nodded for one of the guards to open the door. Wellfall hoped that he had stalled long enough for Lee Powell to decide what they were going to do.

"If you will follow me?" he said.

"Only too happy to."

Wellfall appeared nervous.

Suddenly, Kearny was enjoying himself immensely.

Clint was not sure when the drumbeat began.

He was hiding in the shadows, biding his time before pressing deeper into the cave, when skilled human hands began playing the stretched leather surfaces of drums. Clint Adams did not recognize it as a voodoo beat.

Suddenly, the cave seemed a very different place—the shadows deeper and stranger—and his position there even more precarious. At least the bleeding from his nose and ears had stopped, and there did not seem to be any permanent damage from it.

Just then, passing in front of him, he saw two very tall, lean white men dressed in garish rags of Jamaican villagers. From the odd look in their eyes it was easy to see that they were under some kind of hypnotic spell.

Clint decided to follow them, sensing that they would lead him to what he hoped to find.

Pushing away from the darkness, he took after them, staying far enough behind that he could duck into shadows if he needed to.

The cave was incredibly big, a maze of right turns and dead ends that the two white men avoided instinctively. Obviously they knew the cave well, were a part of its lifestyle, down here.

The drums grew louder.

Since the initial scream Clint had not heard another, but that first one still seemed to echo in his ears.

From around a jagged bend came two more white men in the same kind of trance, joining the other two. Neither of the new men even glanced in Clint's direction.

Clint started to wonder if they would see him even if he was to jump in front of them. He also had the impression that these men in hypnotic trances were somehow being summoned by the drums.

The four men proceeded along a straight and narrow corridor to what appeared to be a large opening in the cave wall.

Clint allowed the men to precede him by more than a few feet. He moved to the opening, stopped behind a craggy chunk of rock, and watched them.

The steady pounding of the drum seemed to insinuate itself into his body. He felt that if he let himself go he could easily fall under its spell and lose his will like the other four men.

Clint started to believe more and more what Kate O'Hara had told him about mind control, but he still refused to believe that it was something . . . magic! If a man were weak-willed enough to allow his mind to be controlled, that was his own fault, and not the result of any supernatural influence.

Clint leaned further into the opening to get a better look. He saw the most amazing thing he'd yet laid eyes on in Reverend Wellfall's castle.

He was about to try to get closer for a better look when his foot accidentally kicked a piece of loose shale over the edge of the opening. He saw the white rock drop many yards below into a pit. Only seconds after the splash several long, lizard-like creatures slithered from the mud bank of the pit into the water.

Clint had never seen such creatures in the west before, but he had seen them during a trip he had taken to South America several years before.

Crocodiles!

Clint stepped through the opening and found himself facing a small chasm. To follow the four men further, he had to leap the chasm, with the crocodiles waiting below for him to make a wrong move. Still, if the stiff moving, trance-like men had leaped it before him, he didn't think he'd have any trouble.

He leaped and landed cat-like on the other side and immediately ran behind a huge outcrop of rock to hide before looking below.

Moments later, easing himself out around the outcrop he saw below a natural bowl carved out of rock.

Within this bowl sat at least fifty white men who looked as if they were all drunk on the same exotic wine. In the center of a circle formed by them was a pagan altar not unlike the one he had seen on the upper floor.

To the right of the altar a short black man in a yellow shirt and torn red pants banged hypnotically on his drum while the rest of the men took up a monotonous chant. Nearby, several women, a few of whom Clint recognized as being part of the castle staff, danced in a lusty frenzy to the musical beat, their mostly naked bodies shining with sweat and oils in the licking flame of the lanterns. Among them Clint saw the well-endowed young woman who had come to his room and offered herself to him.

Finally, Clint returned his gaze to the altar. Something about it seemed familiar—something more than just its resemblance to the slab of stone upstairs.

He looked more closely at the naked female form resting there, apparently ready for sacrifice, as the women danced around it.

Then he realized why the form looked so familiar.

The naked woman was Kate O'Hara!

TWENTY-SEVEN

"Oh, my God," Senator Selkirk said.

He was lying face down on his bed while the woman who had joined him earlier—Darla—massaged his fleshy body.

Occasionally, she let her hand drop to prod his cock into an erection.

She had been doing that now for the past five minutes and Selkirk felt as if he were about to lose his mind with ecstacy.

It was because of his preoccupation with his own pleasures that he did not notice the man with the voodoo doll emerge from behind the curtains of his room.

"So, as you can plainly see," Reverend Wellfall said, showing the empty dining room to Lt. Kearny, "there is nobody up at this hour. My followers come here to be healed of their woes—and this means leading a healthy life."

Kearny, who had heard rumors of the endless partying that went on within these walls, had to work hard to keep from smiling.

"Shall we continue on?"

Reverend Wellfall looked offended by the policeman's belligerent tone.

"Of course. This way . . ."

"Please," Senator Selkirk said.

The full-bodied blonde woman had rolled him over onto his back, her big, voluptuous breasts spilling out of her skimpy dress.

Selkirk's mouth began to water.

He reached up to cup one of her breasts.

"Please," he said again, pulling her down to him.

She gladdened him by getting on the bed with him and straddling him, her groin directly over his while he filled his mouth with her luscious breasts.

Still unbeknownst to Selkirk, the voodoo man who had emerged from behind the curtain raised the tiny doll so that it was bathed in the moonlight from the window.

The doll, fashioned in the image of Selkirk, seemed to draw life from the direct contact with the moonbeam.

It seemed to wriggle in the voodoo man's hand.

Selkirk had reached beneath the skirt of the young woman on top of him and was feeling the hot, moist juices which flowed from her pussy.

He licked his lips, hungrily.

He was so enraptured that he did not see the woman remove a small amount of powder from a vial and place it on her tongue. She moved away from his probing, insistent hand then and brought her lips down to his. She kissed him, driving her tongue deep into his mouth, cupping his face on both sides with her hands. Her tongue, poking into his mouth—tasting slightly bitter—seemed to be reaching all the way down to his groin. Slowly, she ran her mouth down over his chin, his neck, his flabby chest, his pot belly until her nose was tangled in the hair at his crotch. His cock was standing straight and tall, an erection like none he'd ever had before, and she opened her mouth and slid her lips over him, taking him inside.

In that moment, he was hers!

The voodoo man took a long straight pin from his shirt pocket and jabbed it into the center of the doll's heart.

Selkirk's body stiffened, his hands fell away from the woman's head and he gave a shriek that caused even the voodoo man to wince.

Clint's first impulse on seeing the helpless form of Kate O'Hara on the pagan slab of the altar was to rush down to her aid.

He quelled that desire and watched, knowing that he would have no chance down there against a force of mind controlled men. Wondering if he had time to go for help, he turned and saw a fleshy white man about to put an axe into the back of his head.

"Take him," the voodoo man told the blonde woman, who still had Selkirk's rigid penis in her mouth. "Sit him up."

She released him and took hold of the Senator's shoulders.

The voodoo man went over to Selkirk and snapped his fingers in front of the older man's face.

Selkirk sat with his eyes open but the snapping fingers did not cause him to blink even once.

"Good," the man said. "Now we can take him downstairs."

"I wish there was something we could do," the fiery young reporter named Gretchen said as she paced the floor of Swami Jack's room. "He should have been back by now."

"Relax," said Swami Jack. "Clint will be all right."

She studied Swami Jack carefully.

"You don't really believe that, do you?" Her tone accused him.

Swami Jack Dolan, still resplendent in his robes, although they were somewhat charred, said, "No."

TWENTY-EIGHT

Clint moved just in time to avert the axe.

He ducked to the right.

The axe *panged* off solid rock.

Clint put his fist into the thick waist of the man and then turned and leaped across the chasm at the bottom of which the hungry crocs prowled.

Clint needed to get back to Swami Jack and work out some sort of plan. He did not believe that Kate was in any immediate danger of being killed, because once Lee Powell discovered that Clint was alive, finding him would be the black man's main concern. He would not carry out a sacrifice without first capturing Clint, again.

Clint knew he was going to have to search this vast cave until he found a way of getting back to the upper level, while avoiding the gas filled room.

He decided not to think of just how long that could take.

As they passed down a narrow passageway whose walls were filled with displays of hand weapons dating from the seventeenth century, Lt. Kearny felt the tip of his nose begin to itch, as if he were about to sneeze.

Reverend Wellfall paused, nodded for one of the guards to throw open a door.

"In here we have an enclosed courtyard," the Reverend said proudly.

Tables for two sat empty.

"As you can see," the Reverend said, "no one is here."

Kearny sneezed.

"God bless you," Wellfall said with some amusement.

"I hope He will."

"Are you ready to go, Lieutenant? It is getting very late."

Kearny wasn't ready to go, but he knew he would have to. The search had been a farce, but he was only one man, and he did not have free reign. Nailing Wellfall on something would have to come another day.

"I'm ready."

Clint's luck changed abruptly for the better as he found a winding stairway that ended at a door leading to the castle's kitchen.

He opened it carefully, listened for any sounds, and then snuck into the huge, white room filled with ovens and glistening pots and pans.

The staff had apparently retired for the night.

He found the hallway and headed back to Swami Jack's room, hoping that Kate O'Hara was still alive, and would stay that way until he could return for her.

This time when Lt. Kearny sneezed he received no blessing from Reverend Wellfall, just an annoyed look. Good, Kearny thought, if I'm annoying him then at least I'll win a small victory.

By now, however, he had begun to understand why he was sneezing. Earlier that night, when he had first been called to the hospital on the matter of the missing woman, he found that the residue of the woman's perfume in her room was strong enough to aggravate his formidable allergies.

He had sneezed a great deal while in the hospital room.

And he was sneezing again.

Which told him one thing.

That the woman had been taken from the hospital and brought here, and had passed through this very corridor. She was in the castle somewhere, being held against her will.

For what purpose?

The Reverend, Kearny and the guards had encircled the entire first floor of the castle and were on their way back to the Reverend's den.

The Reverend held the door open.

"As you can see," he said, smiling with great satisfaction, "she is not here."

Kearny smiled, too, wanting to see the shock on the other man's face. He did not enter the den, but spoke from the corridor.

"I disagree," he said. "My nose tells me that she is here. I'll be back with more men, Reverend. You can count on that."

At that point the tall black man, Lee Powell, strode from the den and said to the guards, "Seize him!"

Before Kearny could move his arms were pinned to his sides. He stopped smiling.

TWENTY-NINE

On her way back to her room to freshen up Gretchen passed beneath a balcony. Something stirred above her.

Frightened, the events of the long night wearing on her now, Gretchen fled past the balcony into the adjacent hallway.

There, clinging to the shadows, she looked back at the balcony to see what had made the noise.

After a time, Ben Tolliver appeared.

He no longer resembled the nondescript man who had been rescued from drowning this afternoon by the Gunsmith.

Indeed, Tolliver was now quite a different man. For one thing he was clad entirely in black. For another he wore two guns strapped very low, the way she had seen gunfighters wear them. And finally, the man kept whipping his guns out with amazing speed, and then jammed them back into his holsters only to do it again. He would shake his head or nod after each draw, and she knew that he was practicing. For a few moments she watched, fascinated.

Then, mysteriously, Tolliver went back into the room where the balcony led—his room, Gretchen realized.

She hurried to her own small room, still thinking about the strange spectacle Tolliver had presented.

Why would Ben Tolliver be preparing himself for some kind of gunfight?

Lee Powell watched as the gas was sucked back into the wall through vents. He wore a mask of rubber which made his gauntness all the more eerie.

He was waiting until he could catch sight of the dead body of the "priest".

When the last of the gas was cleared, and after he had circled the room again and again in disbelief, he stormed out into the hall.

"Guards!" he shouted after whipping off the rubber mask.

The two guards came running, guns drawn.

"Search the castle at once," he told them angrily. "Get some more men to help you. You remember the priest. Find him and bring him to me—and I don't care if he's alive or dead."

"Yes, sir."

Neither man could recall having ever seen Powell

quite this angry. They also noticed something else about the man, something in his eyes they'd never seen before.

Just a hint of fear.

After the guards left Lee Powell went over to the altar. He looked directly at it for the first time and saw that the lid had been opened. So that's where he escaped to, down the steps before the gas had been able to kill him.

Down to the lower level, where Kate O'Hara and the policeman Kearny were presently being held.

Nothing could be done with either of them, however, until the fake priest was found. They had to make sure that the man did not escape the castle and bring back help.

Nothing was going to interfere with his plans.

Nothing . . . and no one.

Swami Jack Dolan tried to stay awake as long as he could but he finally dozed off sitting in a chair by the window.

Around 3 a.m. he was startled from his slumber by a gentle knocking on his door.

Could it be the black man, or some guards? Or was it lovely Gretchen, coming back to while away the small hours of the night?

You should be so lucky, Dolan, he thought as he rose to answer the door.

When he opened it he saw Clint Adams standing there. As the man rushed past him Dolan turned and exclaimed, "Clint!"

"Close the door!"

The portly bishop complied and then turned to face the Gunsmith. Clint had already walked to the basin water in Swami Jack's room and was using the water and towel to clean dried blood from his nose, ears, face and neck.

"We were afraid you were dead."

"Who's we?"

"Gretchen. She's really a reporter for a New York newspaper, Clint, planning to expose Wellfall and his religion."

Clint dried his face, then blew his nose into the towel several times to clear his nasal passages of dried blood.

"She knows about us?" he asked, throwing the towel away.

"She recognized you."

He hesitated only a moment before saying, "All right, then, she can help, too."

"Help with what?"

"Listen," Clint said, and began to explain a plan that had been evolving in his mind.

THIRTY

Gretchen, unable to sleep, convinced now more than ever that there was a story within these walls that would make her the most famous—and wealthiest—female reporter in the United States, set out from her room at about the same time Clint was unveiling his plan. She made her way through the darkness towards the Reverend's den, where Wellfall spent a good portion of his time. She was hoping to get inside and see what the papers on his desk would tell her.

When she reached the door she pressed her ear against it and waited.

Nothing.

The den was empty.

She tried the doorknob and it turned easily. She opened the door and slipped inside.

Moonlight fell across the massive desk, painting everything on it a smooth silver. She immediately went to the drawers and began to open them.

It was in this position, with her back to the door, bent over an open drawer, that she was in when a kerosene lamp suddenly sprayed light through the room and Lee Powell entered.

Clint had dispatched Swami Jack to Gretchen's room to bring her back so that they could work her into the plan, but he knew something was wrong from the look on Jack's face when he returned—without the girl.

"She's not in her room."

"Where could she have gone?"

"From what I know of her I'd say she's snooping around the castle."

"And she'll probably get herself in trouble, and we've got one woman to rescue already. Well, there's nothing we can do but hope she's safe," Clint said. Moving for the door he said to his dubious accomplice, "Let's go . . ."

Swami Jack followed, muttering, "This is worse than setting myself on fire—and that was crazy!"

In his dreams Tolliver strode down the dusty western street at exactly noon.

He was dressed all in black.

He had only this morning gotten himself a shave and haircut. He looked good enough that the ladies among the onlookers on each side of the street smiled as he passed them.

"Be careful!" one of them called. "So you can call on me tonight!"

But now was not the time to be thinking about calling on beautiful women and taking them to bed.

There was a task at hand.

A man, a real man, had to embrace his fate and that was what Ben Tolliver was doing here.

From the other end of the street came the man known as Clint Adams, the Gunsmith.

He looked every bit as serious as Tolliver.

Even in his dream Tolliver felt his gut wrench tightly.

He felt the sweat collect in puddles in his hand-tooled boots and under his armpits.

Scared.

No doubt about it.

Terrified.

The weight of his guns seemed enormous all of a sudden. He wanted to empty his holsters of them, empty the bullets into the Gunsmith's body.

The Gunsmith stopped.

So did Tolliver.

The men were within range of one another now.

It was time.

In just a few more seconds his fierce reputation would be won back, in spades!

He had been a coward once, true, but no more. He was going to prove himself today.

Then he saw the Gunsmith draw.

Sunlight played off of the Gunsmith's gun, giving the weapon a molten look.

Instinctively, Tolliver drew.

Gunfire barked.

And the Gunsmith killed him . . .

Tolliver, bathed in sweat, woke up.

For a wild moment he could not shake himself free of the dream. His hands felt his body for bullet holes, and then he dropped his hands, feeling foolish and drained.

It wasn't going to happen that way in real life.

He wouldn't let it.

He knew exactly how he would kill Clint Adams.

A way that guaranteed that the Gunsmith wouldn't have a chance.

They stripped Gretchen, baring her wonderful breasts —taking the time to fondle them roughly—and then strapped her in a chair and left her in the darkness of the Reverend's den.

She was sore from the beating Lee Powell had instructed the two guards to give her.

Suddenly, she realized that she wasn't alone in the dark room.

Something cold slithered across her foot.

Snakes.

From a tiny spyhole in the wall Lee Powell watched the room where Gretchen sat.

In the past hour the guards had turned up nothing in their search for the fake priest. The guards on all exits from the castle were all in place and had not seen him. That meant he was still loose somewhere in the castle.

There had been one interesting development, however, and that had been catching this beautiful young woman in the Reverend's den.

What was she doing there?

What had she been looking for?

She had refused to answer, and Lee Powell had her beaten and humiliated just short of rape, yet still she wouldn't talk. A courageous young woman—but he knew how to deal with brave women like her.

Lee Powell knew now that when the snakes finally broke her he'd know a lot more about the phony priest than he did now—much more.

And he knew it wouldn't be long before she would be begging to tell him.

He had put a half a dozen snakes of various varieties in the room with her. They would be drawn to the warmth of her body. Perhaps one of them would even slither up her body and slide itself between her warm, cushiony breasts.

Soon she would be begging.

Pleading.

She'd tell him *anything*.

He smiled and waited.

He wondered what she would say if she knew that none of the snakes were poisonous.

THIRTY-ONE

Clint said, "Looks like I'm going to need one more disguise."

"It'll never work, Clint," Swami Jack Dolan argued anxiously.

"Sure it will," Clint said, with more assurance than he felt. "Besides, it's our only chance. Lee Powell controls them. Maybe somebody else can take over—for a while."

"What if they find out that you're a fake?"

"Then they'll kill me."

"You're willing to face that?"

"Kate O'Hara's down there, Jack."

"You think she's still alive?"

"I hope she is. I'm hoping they won't dare kill her until they catch me."

"Speaking of which, why haven't they been here looking for you?"

They were in Swami Jack's room.

"The only thing I can figure is that they think I'd never be dumb enough to come back here. We've got to get out of here before they change their minds. Come on, Swami Jack, do your stuff," Clint said, pulling off the phony beard. "Help me get ready."

Kate O'Hara came back to consciousness.

She lay on a cot, a blanket thrown over her.

She sensed she wasn't alone.

Startled, she started up from her cot but the pain in her shoulder coupled with the man's hand on her good shoulder changed her mind.

What was most crazy about the moment—what gave the scene a bit of a dream feel—was that the man was wearing a hat.

A homburg.

"Just relax, Miss O'Hara. I'm a friend."

"How did you know my name?"

"You were abducted from your hospital room tonight. You have a bandage on your shoulder."

"Who are you?"

He doffed his homburg, as if they were just meeting in the street, or at a social.

"I am Lieutenant Kearny. I've been working on finding who shot you, and then on where you disappeared to."

She looked helplessly around the cell. She could not

quite clear her head and felt as if she wanted to go back to sleep.

"You've come to rescue me, then?"

"Yes," he said, "and I've done a bang-up job of it, haven't I?"

It took her fifteen minutes to start screaming, which impressed Lee Powell.

Obviously this woman was a brave one. Most people —men or women—would have started screaming long before the snakes had coiled themselves around them.

She'd held out this long.

Quite impressive.

He threw open the door, a long bar of light preceding him and chasing the snakes, who slithered off to find dark corners.

He stood over her and smirked.

There was a madness in her eyes now and he knew that she would be cooperative.

He picked up one of the slower-moving reptiles and let it coil itself around his arm.

Gretchen put her head down, not wanting to watch.

She had no strength or resistance left.

None at all.

Just minutes after she finished telling Lee Powell what he wanted to know, Gretchen put her head down on her chest and passed into unconsciousness.

Lee Powell uncoiled the harmless yet ugly reptile from his arm, dropped it to the floor and then walked to the door to call for two guards.

"Take her downstairs with the others," he said, and left the room quickly.

THIRTY-TWO

"Jim West? The Secret Service agent?"

"One and the same," Lee Powell said.

They were in Wellfall's room, Powell having just awakened the Reverend and given him the news he'd gotten from the girl, Gretchen.

In disbelief Wellfall repeated the information.

"The 'priest' is actually the Gunsmith, working for Jim West?"

"Exactly."

"And this girl is a newspaper reporter?"

"Correct."

"My God," Wellfall said, running his hands over his face nervously.

"Something will have to be done, and quickly."

"Yes, something will have to be done," Wellfall agreed quickly, "but what?"

Slowly, Lee Powell said, "We will have to put some of our theories to the test."

"Meaning what?"

"Meaning that we will actually have to see if we can control Selkirk—see if we can't get him to do something insane that will rid us of the Gunsmith and company and remove us from all possible blame at the same time."

"But what a waste," Wellfall said, standing up. "Selkirk was all set up—"

"We can get someone else."

"I hope you've thought this through, Lee."

Powell looked at Wellfall with a mixture of anger and contempt. The minister had taken Powell in upon his arrival to this country, but it was actually because of Powell that Wellfall wasn't still working storefront missions.

"I will have to do things my way."

"If you're sure—"

"I'm sure, most sure."

The Reverend stopped pacing and looked at the black man. He too was aware that their relationship had changed, but he had ceased worrying about who was the master and who was the slave. When their plan worked, they'd both be powerful and wealthy beyond their dreams.

"It could all come crashing down around us, couldn't it, Lee?"

"If we let it, if we do not move quickly to see that it doesn't."

The Reverend glanced around his opulent room and said, "I would hate to have to leave here."

"Believe me, if we do not take care of it you would not only leave here, but you would spend many years in a prison cell for treason."

The Reverend seemed to suffer a chill.

"I've heard stories about prison."

"Unfortunately, most of them are true."

Wellfall eyed the wine bottle on a sideboard by the window and said, "Very well, do what you must."

"I'll have to have the guards continue to search for the Gunsmith and his accomplice."

"You think the Bishop is a phony, too?"

"Of course."

"Have you checked their rooms?"

Powell looked annoyed. Had his men checked their rooms?

"They wouldn't be that foolish," he said, uncomfortably.

"They might. Where else could they go?"

"I must go and see to many things," Powell said, moving to the door.

He noticed Reverend Wellfall looking at the wine bottle and said, "Have a glass of wine, Reverend. It will rid you of your chill."

The white men, moving so slowly you suspected they were made of clay, threw Gretchen in with Kate O'Hara and Lieutenant Kearny.

"I told them," Gretchen said, beside herself with guilt and misery.

"Told them what?" Kearny asked.

Gretchen explained to Kearny everything she'd told Lee Powell.

"Well," he said, "that explains a lot—except for one thing."

"What's that?"

"How do we get out of here?"

The tall, pale man with darkened rings beneath his eyes shuffled down the corridor leading to the kitchen. He passed among the pots and pans, in the direction of the door that led to the subterranean level below.

His eyes registered only a minimal form of life.

He was one of them.

A zombie.

Following a few feet behind the man, all the way up to the door, was Swami Jack Dolan. He had discarded his bishop's robe and his bishop's belly, and now stood clad in normal clothes, a medium-sized, slender man.

When the pale man got to the door, opened it and proceeded through, Swami Jack smiled to himself and shook his head.

"I've got to say, Clint," he said to himself, "you'd fool me if I didn't know any better."

The zombie who was the Gunsmith descended the steep and curving staircase, on the way to join the others of his kind who prowled the myriad labyrinth of tunnels beneath the castle.

The ones who would probably tear him limb from limb if they found out that he was not really one of them, at all.

Part of the plan was for Swami Jack Dolan to follow

Clint and be on hand when the phony-priest-turned-zombie made his move. Unfortunately, before Swami Jack could enter the kitchen he was seized from behind by two sets of vice-like hands.

And the Gunsmith was on his own.

THIRTY-THREE

Wellfall was having breakfast on his enclosed balcony when Lee Powell appeared.

"What's the news? Have you found the Gunsmith?"

"No, but we have his friend."

Powell explained how his guards had gone to the Bishop's room, found the red robes and some padding that had obviously been worn beneath it to provide for some extra girth.

"They found him entering the kitchen."

"The kitchen?"

"He was obviously looking for a way to get downstairs. They took him because he was a stranger, but when I saw him I knew he was the same man who played at being the bishop."

"And?" Wellfall was anxious. "Did he tell you where Clint Adams is?"

"No, but he will. First, we must talk."

"About what?"

"About Senator Selkirk."

"And what about this Gunsmith? What are you going to do about him?"

"My guards on the grounds assured me that no one got through them during the night. We may not know where Adams is, but he is still on the grounds. He can't escape."

"And what about Selkirk?"

"He's going to kill two women and two men," Powell said, "right in front of dozens of witnesses—and one of the men will be a policeman."

"My God. Kearny?"

"Yes. And the Secret Service woman, the reporter, and the 'bishop'. He will then be apprehended by two of our people, and he will be killed trying to escape."

"Can you get him to do it?"

"Yes."

The white zombies who roamed the passages below the castle were at one time help here in the castle—cowboys down on their luck, drifters with no ties. Giving them potions and keeping them under control had not been difficult.

Now the Jamaican had to do something more difficult, however. He had to take the mind of an intelligent man, a politician, and bend it to his own will.

Powell knew that, to date, with all the experiments with hypnosis—most notably by a man named Mesmer in Europe—not one of the subjects had been able to violate their basic moral principles while under the influence.

They had not been able to kill.

Powell felt that he had the power to overcome that, with Senator Selkirk as his subject.

"That saves our necks, all right—*if* you can take care of the Gunsmith."

"He'll be taken care of," Powell said, with conviction. "If he is around he will try and save his friends—and then we'll have him."

"And what of our plans to seize control of the government? With Selkirk dead, we'll suffer a major setback—"

"There will be an empty seat in the Senate," Lee Powell said. "You can have something to say about who will fill it. I do not think we will be set back all that far."

No, Wellfall thought, not as long as six people died.

When the man was thrown into the dank cell with Kearny, Gretchen and the unconscious Kate O'Hara, the policeman recognized him upon untying him and removing the gag from his mouth.

"Swami Jack!"

"Who?" Gretchen asked.

"A common con man."

Gretchen narrowed her eyes and studied Swami Jack's face and then exclaimed, "The bishop!"

"Impersonating men of the cloth now, are you, Jack?" Kearny asked. He looked at Gretchen and said,

"Just my luck. I'm going to die along with the likes of him."

"I'm not such a bad fellow," Swami Jack said as Gretchen untied his hands.

"Where's Clint?" she asked.

"I don't know."

"Didn't they ask you?"

"They asked me, but they didn't torture me. That's where I thought they were taking me when they threw me in here."

The knot came loose and he pulled his hands free, massaging his wrists.

"Thank you, Gretchen."

"They probably have something else to attend to before questioning you."

"Yeah, but what?"

"Finding Adams, naturally," Kearny said.

"It may be something bigger than that," Gretchen said.

"Like what?" the policeman asked.

"Like something involving Senator Selkirk. He must be here for a reason."

"Maybe so," Kearny said, "but we won't be finding out about it. Not from down here."

"Maybe Clint will find us and get us out of here," Swami Jack said, hopefully.

"I'm afraid that's nothing more than wishful thinking," Kearny said. "He's probably preoccupied with keeping himself alive."

"Maybe not."

"You do know where he is, don't you?" Gretchen asked.

"Not exactly. All I know is that he's down here,

someplace, looking for her." He indicated Kate
O'Hara, who was still unconscious on the cot and not
looking very well.

"And who is she? What does she have to do with all
of this?"

"She's Secret Service."

"Christ, her, too?" Kearny exploded. "Why wasn't I
told about any of this?"

Swami Jack shrugged and said, "You'd probably
have to talk to the President about that."

"I'd talk to the Devil himself and like it if it would get
us out of here."

"It would take him to do it, too," Gretchen said, and
no one in the cell argued with her.

THIRTY-FOUR

After following some of the entranced, pale men around for some time Clint soon realized the reasons and the purpose for their existence.

This subterranean maze—upon which the castle had probably deliberately been built—was where Lee Powell conducted various kinds of experiments. The white zombies were one form of experiment. Every half hour or so they'd stop by niches carved in the walls where bowls of white granules waited for them. A drug of some kind, of course. This was *how* he controlled them.

Why he controlled them was simple: They performed all the menial tasks down here, served as jailers, as mules. He had indoctrinated them in the ways of voo-doo, rendering them total slaves.

Presently, Clint Adams moved among them, pretend-ing to be in a slave-like trance, moving as slow and as stiffly as they moved in an attempt to simply blend in.

He was handed a broom. He swept a section of the corridor. Next he was handed a bucket of human excre-ment, apparently taken from the cells. He took it to a hole in a wall on the other side of which he could hear running water. He dumped the stuff into the hole, where it would be carried away by the water.

As he finished his task he heard a scuffle behind him and turned to find three of the pale zombies grabbing a man who was not so pale. Clint suspected that the drug did not work the same way on everyone, and even here there was prejudice. If you were not as much a white zombie as the rest of the white zombies, you were discriminated against.

Which is what these people were doing right now—dragging off an "inferior" male.

But to where?

Clint checked himself quickly, making sure that the chalky mixture Swami Jack had applied to his skin made him look sufficiently like the other zombies.

The pitiful man struggled against the others, but to no avail. When his struggles became an annoyance they simply smashed his head against a rock, splitting it open like an overripe melon.

Holding the man in their arms like so much kindling now they walked into one of the tunnels, and Clint followed. Soon enough he began to realize where they were going.

They came to the banks he had seen from above—the banks where the crocodiles lay.

The area reeked so much that Clint had to fight to

keep from gagging aloud. Obviously this was their feeding ground, where Lee Powell disposed of his failed experiments. The stench was that of rotting human meat.

They took the man and threw him into the water.

The crocs quickly slithered off the banks and into the water where the man had been tossed. He looked as if he were simply a drowning man, and the movement had attracted the hungry creatures.

Swiftly, the crocodiles struck, and in less than a minute they had totally dismembered the body. They each took their chunk of human meat back to the banks with them, and fed contentedly.

Clint watched them as long as he could and was about to turn away when suddenly a heavy hand descended on his shoulder. He turned around and stared at the biggest zombie he had seen yet.

The man was frowning at him, and Clint simply stared back without expression, trying to brazen it out. Obviously, this big sonofabitch had some doubts about Clint, and he quickly devised his own test.

With his big hand holding tight to Clint's shoulder the man pulled the Gunsmith over to a wall where some white granules could be found. He seemed to want Clint to scoop some of them up and either inhale them or ingest them.

Clint knew that he dared not do either, or his pretense of being a zombie would cease being a pretense.

Unsatisfied with Clint's reaction the zombie cupped his hands, scooped up some of the granules and raised the stuff to Clint's face. Clint dimly became aware that some of the other zombies had come over and formed a ring around him and the larger man.

What the hell was he going to do now?

THIRTY-FIVE

Kate O'Hara came awake suddenly and the others crowded around her as she filled them in on what she and Clint Adams had been trying to do.

"Mind control," Kearny said, scoffing. "It sounds more like mind*less* drivel. I'm more concerned with why I was kept in the dark."

"Those were our orders, Lieutenant," Kate said, weakly. "We had no choice."

"Seems to me that if we had been working together from the beginning we might not be in this mess now."

Kate put a hand to her forehead, frowning, and said, "You may be right."

"She shouldn't be talking," Gretchen said to Kearny. She put a concerned hand on Kate's arm and said, "She should be in the hospital with that wound."

"You're absolutely right," Kearny said. "You shouldn't even have the strength to be walking around, young lady. I admire you."

"I don't understand a lot of what's happening," Kate complained. "I black out, I wake up—"

She was interrupted by the sound of the key being inserted into the door. Kearny stood up, as did Gretchen. Kate O'Hara remained on the cot, while Swami Jack tried to find a corner to hide in.

Two of Lee Powell's mind-controlled—or hypnotised —white slaves entered and gestured to Kate.

"She can't get up!" Gretchen said to them.

They moved towards the wounded young woman and it was plain that they meant to pick her up. Kearny tried to get between them, but both of the men lifted him and tossed him aside like a bag of grain. The policeman struck the wall with painful force and sat on the floor, stunned.

Next Gretchen tried to protect Kate, but one of the men simply swept her aside with his arm.

They stopped then, the two zombies, and looked at Swami Jack, as if asking if he was going to try and stop them, as well. Swami Jack saw no real point in having himself tossed against the wall like the policeman, so he merely held his hands up and shrugged.

The two men grabbed Kate O'Hara, lifted her up and one of them tossed her over his shoulder with ease. Then they left the cell, slamming the door behind them.

Kearny staggered to his feet and helped Gretchen up, assisting her to the cot. Then he turned angrily on Swami Jack.

"Where were you?"

"I didn't see any point in having my head handed to me for nothing."

"Of course not. You care only about yourself."

"Leave him alone," Gretchen said, wearily. "If that were true, he wouldn't be here at all."

"He still should have tried to help that poor girl."

"He wouldn't have been any more effective than you or I was."

Kearny grunted, but backed off.

"I wonder why they split us up?" Gretchen asked. "And where they're taking her?"

"I don't know," Kearny said, "and I'm trying not to think about it."

It was near dawn when Ben Tolliver heard the commotion out in the hall. It sounded like many footsteps, running back and forth. He rose, dressed, checked and made sure that his guns were secured underneath his mattress, and then stepped out into the hallway.

As he stepped out he was almost run into by two of Reverend Wellfall's guards.

"What's wrong?" asked one. "What's going on?"

"We suggest you stay in your room for a few more hours, sir," one of them said. "Everything should be cleared up by then."

"What should be cleared up?"

"I'm afraid we'll just have to ask you to step back into your room," the second guard said, and both of them moved towards him so that he had two choices: be squashed between them and the door or open the door and go back into his room.

Inside, he frowned, wondering what all the commotion was about. Suddenly, he was overcome by a feeling of dread. Somehow, he had the feeling that the Gunsmith was involved in this. He was, after all, pretending to be a priest.

If they were searching for the Gunsmith, they might kill him when they found him, and then his chance to redeem himself would be gone.

He quickly pulled his guns out from beneath the mattress, strapped them on and moved to the door.

He had to find Clint Adams before they did—and kill him!

THIRTY-SIX

Lee Powell pressed his head against the chest of Senator Thomas Selkirk. At first there was no evidence of heartbeat whatsoever. He pressed his ear tighter against the man's flabby chest, fearful for a moment that he had actually killed him.

Finally, a heartbeat throbbed through the Senator's fleshy torso. It was very faint, but it was there.

Powell stepped away from the altar where the Senator lay and picked up a Devil's mask lying nearby.

At that moment the two huge doors leading to the hall opened and two of Lee Powell's zombies entered. Reverend Wellfall, who had been watching the activities at the altar intently, turned and saw that one of the men had Kate O'Hara slung over his shoulder.

"Why is she here?" Wellfall asked. "Are you going to have him kill her now?"

"No," Powell said, giving Wellfall an annoyed look for interrupting. "I will explain."

Powell slipped the Devil mask over his face. In the eerie green light he looked terrifying.

He began muttering the ancient voodoo exhortations needed to take control of somebody's soul and body.

Selkirk was useless for their practical purposes now, but he was still Powell's greatest experiment.

He dared not fail.

Clint looked around at the circle of zombies around him. Pathetic half-men, their minds long ago burnt out by the very substance they were now trying to get the Gunsmith to ingest.

He had only one chance that he could see, and he grabbed it with both hands.

He scooped a good portion of the white granules out of the other man's hands. He did not know if the drug could be absorbed through his skin, but he was betting his life that it couldn't.

Closing his eyes tightly and drawing his lips into his mouth, hiding them, he plunged his face into his hands and began to rub the stuff on himself, holding his breath.

He took a long time doing this, hoping that the others would be satisfied and get bored with watching him, and when he looked up he saw that many of them had wandered away. Soon, only the big one was left, still holding some of the granules in his own hands. Slowly, he brought his hands up to his face, inhaled deeply and then just stood there, a euphoric expression on his face. The look resembled one that Clint had seen in the opium dens of Chinatown, in San Francisco.

Clint tried to copy that look, pretending to inhale again, and then the big man simply turned and started to walk away.

Clint opened his hands and let the granules fall to the ground. When he was sure he wasn't being observed he vigorously rubbed his face, trying to get rid of all traces of the stuff.

He fervently wished for a good stiff drink.

Wellfall noticed that Lee Powell had suddenly removed his mask and stood staring at Selkirk.

"What's wrong."

Powell looked at Wellfall and said, "We're too close to give up now."

"What do you mean?"

"I mean I don't want to give up, just yet."

"But Clint Adams, and the Secret Service, and the newspaper bitch—"

"We can take care of all of them ourselves. We have them all but Adams, and as long as we have them, he'll try to rescue them."

"What makes you say that? What makes you think he won't just try to get out and save his own skin?"

Lee Powell shook his head slowly.

"He is a man of great principle, Reverend. He will come for them."

"What about her?"

Kate O'Hara was unaware that the two men were discussing her. She had once again lapsed into unconsciousness, brought on by the presence of Lee Powell's drug, still in her system.

"We will go ahead with our plan," Powell said. "If I can get Selkirk to kill her, then he will be totally under our control."

Reverend Wellfall did some quick thinking and decided that Lee Powell was right. They were too close to give it all up, to set themselves back who knew how long before they could make another try.

"All right, then," Wellfall said, "let's do it."

Suddenly, the corridors had emptied out.

Ben Tolliver didn't understand it. First they were all over the place and now they were gone. *Where* had they gone to? And where were all the rest of the people? Had they all been warned to stay in their rooms? Didn't any of them wonder what was going on?

He began to follow the corridors himself, knowing that if he was caught with his guns he was going to either do a lot of explaining . . . or a lot of shooting.

Eventually, he spotted a lone guard walking along, and decided to simply follow him and see where he took him.

THIRTY-SEVEN

Clint was startled by what he saw.

After cleaning his face off as best he could he once again picked up two or three of his fellow zombies and began to trail them. They led him into an area of the sub-basement that he had not seen before.

Directly ahead of him were several different torture devices, including a rack and a chair to which were strapped electrodes. Behind this area lay four cells, carved out of the rock and fronted by large steel doors with small peepholes.

The zombies went over to the doors and began to

peek into them one by one. Clint could almost imagine them nudging each other, laughing at whoever happened to be inside the cells.

So far Clint had not been able to get his bearings well enough to find his way back to the altar room. He had found the area where he'd first seen Kate O'Hara, but she had not been there.

Perhaps she was in one of these cells.

As the trio of pale men moved away from the first door, Clint walked over to it and looked in.

There was a Mexican man inside who appeared to have been scourged with a whip.

In the next cell was some poor, formerly human beast who had been burned beyond recognition. The most horrible thing about this one was that he—she—it—was still alive!

He watched as the three "friends" moved on past the fourth, obviously empty cell, and then left the area. Clint moved to the third cell and looked in.

"What is your name?"
"Thomas Selkirk."
"Your occupation?"
"I am a United States senator."
Even in his present condition there was an unmistakable tone of pride in his voice.
"Do you know who I am?"
"No."
"I am your Master."
Selkirk said nothing.
"Repeat it."
"You are my Master."
"Do you know why I am here?"
Selkirk hesitated, then said, "No."

"To tell you what to do."

The Senator hesitated a fraction of a second and then said, "To tell me what to do."

"Very good, Senator, very good."

He turned to the two guards who were holding Kate and motioned for them to bring her forward.

The Senator was still lying prone on the altar, so Lee Powell said, "Get up, Senator. Rise to your feet."

The politician obeyed, standing slowly.

"Have you ever killed anyone before?" Lee Powell asked, at the same time holding his hand out to Reverend Wellfall. The Reverend came forward and placed a .45 revolver in the black man's hand.

"Senator? I asked you if you have ever killed anyone?"

"No."

"Why not?"

"I am . . . a man of peace. I abhor violence."

"That is an admirable stand, Senator. Most admirable. Take this."

He thrust the .45 at the Senator, who opened his hand and accepted it without looking at it.

"When I tell you to do something, you will obey me. Is that correct?"

"Yes."

"Say it."

"When you tell me to do something I will obey you."

"Without question."

"Without question."

Powell motioned to the guards to bring the girl even closer.

"Senator, do you see the young lady?"

The Senator looked at Kate O'Hara and said, "Yes."

"I want you to raise your weapon and fire it at her."

"Weapon?"

"The gun in your hand."

For the first time the Senator looked down at the gun in his hand.

"Raise it and fire it at her."

"But . . . that would injure her."

"You're wrong, Senator," Lee Powell said. "It will kill her."

The Senator looked confused.

"Shoot her."

The man looked old and haggard as he stared at the gun in his hand.

"Obey me."

Nothing.

"You will obey me. You have no will of your own, Senator. I am your Master."

"You are my Master."

"Obey me."

"I will obey you."

"Shoot her."

Slowly, the Senator raised the gun and pointed it at Kate O'Hara.

Clint searched the entire torture room and finally came up with a large, rusted key hanging on one of the walls. He went back to the third cell and inserted the key.

It fit.

"By God, I told you he'd come back for us!" Swami Jack Dolan said to Kearny and Gretchen.

"I never doubted it," Gretchen said.

The door swung open and Gretchen threw her arms around Clint's neck.

"You look awful," she said, "but you're a sight for sore eyes."

Clint disengaged himself from her and opened his shirt. Underneath, in his belt, was the Colt New Line. He had not wanted to use it against the zombies when they were trying to force him to inhale the drug, because there were more of them than the 5 shots the gun held. Besides, firing the gun in the caverns would be dangerous.

"I told them you'd come."

"Where did *you* go?" Clint asked the little con man. "You were supposed to be behind me."

"I was until two of the Reverend's guards grabbed me and brought me down here."

"Have any of you seen Kate?"

"She was here with us until a short time ago," Kearny said. "Then they came and took her away."

"To where?"

"We don't know."

"I think I do," Clint said, "but there's only one way I know for sure how to get there."

"How?" Kearny asked.

"Through the castle."

"Well," Kearny said, grabbing a sharp, long handled axe off the stone wall near him, "let's go."

Gretchen took a smaller but no less sharp hand axe and said, "I'm ready. This is going to be one hell of a story. 'I went into battle with the Gunsmith'."

Clint winced and said, "Jesus, you even talk like a reporter." Clint looked at Swami Jack Dolan and said, "Well, Jack?"

Jack sighed and said, "Lead the way. I'm with you."

•   •   •

"Is he going to do it?" Reverend Wellfall asked anxiously.

"Shh!" Lee Powell said, angrily.

"Senator?"

"Yes?"

"Proceed."

With no more urging than that Senator Selkirk aimed and fired the gun at Kate O'Hara.

THIRTY-EIGHT

They were just rounding a large bend—Gretchen, Swami Jack and Lt. Kearny, all following Clint—when they suddenly found themselves facing a wall of zombies.

"They knew you'd come for us," Swami Jack said, "They were waiting."

"Well, they didn't have to wait long, did they?" Clint said. "Lieutenant, I hope you swing a mean axe."

"I guess we're about to find out."

The drugged men began to advance on them.

"How about going back?" Swami Jack asked.

"Look!" Gretchen said then. "Behind us!"

They all turned and looked and there was another wall of white faced men advancing on them from behind.

"All right," Clint said, drawing his gun. "Let me try to clear a path. If they rush us, we'll just have to fight our way through."

"They're empty-handed," Kearny complained.

"They'll kill you just as soon as look at you, Lieutenant."

Kearny set his jaw and said, "All right."

Clint raised his gun and shot one zombie in the chest. As he had expected, the others kept coming. In fact, the one he shot kept coming. The drug must have brought out their strength or something—at least enough to resist a .22 caliber bullet. When he fired again he hit the man in the head, and he went down. Still, the others stepped over him and kept coming.

"When they reach us," he said, firing and hitting another between the eyes, "swing for their heads."

He fired again, and then again, and was down to one last bullet. He knew he wouldn't have time to reload.

"They're coming from behind!" Gretchen screamed.

Both Kearny and Swami Jack moved to meet them, Kearny swinging his axe, and Jack a club he had picked up. Luckily, though the zombies might have been strong, they were very slow and easy to hit.

Clint fired his last bullet, knowing by now that it was useless. As slow as they were, there were just too many of them to fight off. They would outweigh them by sheer force of numbers.

Suddenly, there was a thunderclap. At least, that's what it sounded like in that cavern. When another followed, and then another Clint knew what it was.

Someone was firing a pair of .45s.

Ahead of him he saw one, two, three zombies fall, and the firing continued. He also heard something else. A rumble, and he could feel it beneath his feet. From the roof came a sprinkling of pebbles and sand, and he knew that the echoes of the guns—whosoever's guns they were—was going to bring the roof down on them.

"Let's go," Clint said. "We've got some help."

They charged forward, weapons swinging, fighting off the clawing hands that grabbed for them while who-ever their saviour was kept firing into the zombies from behind. Soon they broke through, with the zombies re-grouping behind them, joined by the second mob.

Clint saw the man with the guns and was surprised to find that it was Ben Tolliver.

Tolliver was reloading and now shouted, "Adams!" and tossed Clint one of the guns.

Clint caught the gun and told the others, "Keep going."

"Clint—" Gretchen said.

"Take her!" Clint told Kearny.

The policeman took her by the arm and pulled her away with him. Tolliver moved past Gretchen, Kearny and Swami Jack and stood beside Clint. Together, they fired into the advancing zombies.

"What the hell is going on here?" Tolliver shouted.

"I'll have to fill you in later," Clint said. "Right now what do you say we bring the house down?"

Clint gestured with the gun he was holding towards the ceiling and Tolliver caught on.

"Right."

They pointed the guns at the ceiling above the zom-bies and fired the remaining rounds into it.

That was all it took.

Suddenly, the roof seemed to split and tons of rock came rushing through, falling on the zombies. Soon the tunnel was so filled with dust that it was impossible to see.

The roof above them creaked and Clint said, "Let's get out of here. The whole thing is going to go."

They turned and ran just as the rock above them gave way. They ran on through the tunnel until they caught up to the others and Clint said, "This way. The stairs to the kitchen are just ahead."

"Where are we going?" Tolliver asked any one of them.

"You'll know when we get there," Swami Jack said.

THIRTY-NINE

The gunshot rang loudly in the cavernous room where Lee Powell and Reverend Wellfall stood watching as Senator Thomas Selkirk, having fired the gun at Kate O'Hara, let the pistol fall to the floor.

The smile on the good Reverend's face told the tale. The implications of what he'd just witnessed were clear.

"It's going to work," he said, almost in awe. "We can control men's minds—intelligent and powerful men's minds. Do you know what that means, Lee?"

"I know."

The Reverend looked at Kate O'Hara then and his face fell.

"Look!" he shouted, pointing.

Not only wasn't the woman dead, but the sound of the shot seemed to have roused her and she was standing on her own, the two guards having released her arms.

"She's not dead!"

"I know."

"But how? I saw him. He fired directly at her."

Lee Powell leaned over, picked up the gun and said, "Blanks."

"Blanks."

"Yes."

"But . . . why?"

"As a sort of a trial run," Lee Powell said, breaking the gun open and ejecting the blank shells. "Now we will load the gun with real bullets and let the Senator do it again—for real, this time."

Now that they were upstairs in the castle and out of the caves they did not have unarmed zombies to deal with, but armed guards. Luckily, the guards were not gathered together as the zombies had been, but scattered about the castle, still searching for Clint. It had been left to the zombies below to take care of him if he showed up to free his friends.

They ran through the corridors of the first floor, feeling the vibrations beneath their feet increase. Torches began to shake loose from the wall as the holders fell from their moorings.

"This whole castle might go from a chain reaction," Kearny said.

"That's what the good Reverend gets for building it

atop a maze of caverns. I'd rather have had it sitting on solid rock, myself."

"Does anybody want to fill me in on what's going on?" Tolliver asked.

"Gretchen," Clint said, "why don't you take up the rear with our friend and hero here and explain it to him."

"All right, Clint."

"Where are you taking us now?" Kearny asked.

"There's a large room on the second floor, behind a set of red doors. Inside there's an altar set up for sacrifices. I think we'll not only find Kate O'Hara there, but Senator Selkirk as well."

"Selkirk. What's he got to do with this. He's as honest a politician as you can find."

"Even honest men have weaknesses, Lieutenant, and from what I've seen while I've been here the Senator's is lovely young women."

"Can't blame him for that."

It was a remark Clint might not expect from the usually grim lieutenant.

"Anyway, whatever Wellfall and this Lee Powell have planned I'm sure it has something to do with the Senator."

"And mind control?"

Clint looked at Kearny in surprise.

"That's it. Who better to have under your control than a powerful politician who might one day even become President of the United States."

"Jesus Christ!" Kearny said. "That's . . . frightening! We've got to stop them."

"That," Clint said as he led them to a stairway to the second floor, "is just what we're going to do."

•   •   •

Lee Powell had reloaded the gun and handed it back to the Senator. Just at that moment a tremor seemed to go through the castle.

"What was that?" Reverend Wellfall said.

"Nothing," Powell said. "It was just a tremor. Let's proceed."

By the time they reached the second floor Tolliver knew what was going on.

At the head of the stairway Clint called a halt to the procession.

"If we encounter any guards now," he said, "we'll have to try and take them quietly. We don't want to alert anyone."

Just then a tremor went through the castle.

"Jesus, if anyone's going to be alerted it'll be by that."

"Maybe it will keep them busy," Clint said. "Let's go, but quietly."

They started down the corridor, which was lit by torches on both walls. Clint's .22, reloaded, was now in Kearny's possession. The .45 was in Clint's hand. Tolliver, the only other armed man, brought up the rear. Swami Jack held the larger axe, and Gretchen the smaller one.

Surprisingly enough they encountered no resistance on the way to the red doors. As they approached the bend in the corridor, however, they became aware of the sound of voices.

"That figures," Clint said.

"What?" Kearny asked.

"Whatever guards are up here are gathered in front of the corridor that leads to the red doors."

"How are we going to take them without shooting?"

"We can't," Clint said. "We'll just have to take them fast and hope we can get through the doors in time. Let me see how many there are."

He moved quietly ahead and stuck his head out just enough for a look. A quick count told him there were six or seven. He hoped there weren't anymore actually standing in front of the doors.

"All right," he said, rejoining the others. "There's about a half a dozen. I've seen worse odds. Gretchen and Swami Jack hang back, the three of us will have to take them," he said, indicating himself, Kearny and Tolliver.

"Fine," Kearny said.

"Tolliver, you've done your part," Clint said. "You can back out any time you want."

"I'm in until the end," Tolliver said. He didn't add that he had his own reasons for wanting to keep the Gunsmith alive.

"Okay," Clint said, thumbing back the hammer on the .45, "let's go."

FORTY

Clint was impressed with Tolliver's handling of his gun. It made the job much easier. The seven men were totally surprised, and were not particularly adept with their guns. Clint, Tolliver and Kearny made every shot count, and it was over in seconds.

"I don't believe it," Kearny said.

"They were just slow," Clint said.

"I mean you two," Kearny said. "I've never seen anyone handle a gun the way you two just did. I don't think I got more than one shot off."

"As long as the job got done," Clint said, looking at

Tolliver. He thought the man was studying him, but couldn't afford to dwell on it. "Let's get moving. They might have heard the shooting in the altar room."

With Clint in the lead they hurried down the hall to the red doors.

The occupants of the cavernous room were totally unaware of what was happening outside.

The two guards were prepared to grab Kate O'Hara if she started to fall or tried to run for it.

Reverend Wellfall was watching Senator Selkirk intently.

Kate O'Hara was too frightened—and too drained —to move. She stood there and waited for death. She almost thought that it would be a relief.

Senator Selkirk lifted the .45 and once again pointed it at Kate O'Hara.

Lee Powell, his heart beating wildly, knew that his experiments were just seconds away from being successful. Once Selkirk shot the woman Powell would know that he could control any man he wanted to, no matter the size or power of his intellect.

They were all frozen in one scant second of time, watching, waiting—

—and then the red doors burst open.

Clint was gratified to see that there were no guards on the red doors. He charged to them and shoved them open, and realized in that instant that neither he nor the other two men had reloaded their weapons. Possibly the only man who had more than one or two shots left was Kearny.

Clint hit the doors with his shoulder and they burst inward. In a split second he took in the tableau before them.

On the altar were Powell and Selkirk, who was pointing a gun at Kate O'Hara. The guards on either side of Kate turned and clawed for their hand guns. Reverend Wellfall turned, saw Clint and gaped in shock and dismay.

"No!" he shouted.

The guards pulled their weapons out and Clint, first through the doors, fired at one of them, striking him in the chest. When he pulled the trigger again the hammer fell on an empty chamber.

Ben Tolliver came up next to him and fired once, the bullet striking the remaining guard in the face, and then the hammer of Tolliver's gun fell on an empty chamber.

Lee Powell, taking all of that in, smiled tightly and said to Selkirk, "Proceed."

"No!" Clint shouted. "Senator!"

He hadn't gone through all of this just to watch helplessly while Selkirk killed Kate.

"Kill her!" Lee Powell commanded.

"Kearny . . ." Clint said, but the policeman was way ahead of him. He pointed the New Line at the Senator and pulled the trigger.

In that same moment, Selkirk turned abruptly, pointed the gun at Lee Powell, and pulled the trigger.

"No—" Powell had time to say before the .45 caliber slug tore through his forehead. It exited from the back of his head, taking brain tissue and bone with it and splattering the altar, which was behind him. The black man fell over backward, arms stretched out, dead on his own altar.

The .22 bullet that Kearny fired struck Selkirk high in

the chest, on the left side, and the Senator staggered back, dropping his gun. He fought to keep his feet, moving like a puppet whose strings were tangled, and then suddenly the strings were cut and he fell to the floor at the base of the altar.

Clint rushed forward in time to catch Kate, who passed out. He caught her before she could hit the floor.

Kearny moved forward, surveying the damage they had done in the room, and then his eyes rested on Senator Selkirk. He ascended the altar to check on the man, but his shot had been true and struck the man in the heart.

"I thought he was going to shoot the girl."

"We all did, Lieutenant," Clint said.

"I killed him for no reason."

"You don't know that," Clint said. "His mind may have just snapped and Powell was his first victim. He might have turned on us next."

"Yes," Kearny said bitterly, "He *might* have . . ."

FORTY-ONE

"With a little sugar, that stuff doesn't taste half bad," Swami Jack Dolan said.

It was three days later and they were all gathered in Lieutenant Kearny's office to sign their statements. Wellfall was in a cell, awaiting the arrival of a federal marshal to take him to Washington to stand trial for treason. The only ones not present were Ben Tolliver and Kate O'Hara . . .

Before they left the castle, Tolliver had pulled Clint aside.

"You know, I came here to kill you."

"Why?"

"I thought it would give me my confidence back, and remove the stigma of cowardice."

"You didn't act like any coward I ever saw down there, Ben."

"I know," Tolliver said. "That's what changed my mind, being able to help you save that woman. It all happened so fast I didn't even realize what odds we were facing."

"It wouldn't have mattered if you had," Clint said. "You still would have done the same thing."

"Thanks, Clint."

When they went back to town Tolliver was given permission to leave town, because his involvement had come late and was almost involuntary—or unavoidable, in any event.

The others were asked to stay while the mess at the castle was cleaned up, and then to come to Kearny's office to sign statements.

Kate O'Hara was excused because she was back in the hospital, where she had spent the past three days fighting for her life . . .

"I don't understand it," the doctor had told Clint after they'd returned her to the hospital. "There's just no way that woman should have been able to leave that bed, let alone go through what you've just explained to me."

"Voodoo," Gretchen had said, and Clint had shaken his head.

"There's nothing magical about it, Gretchen."

"Then explain it."

"Doctor, would a drug have enabled her to ignore her wounds and walk around?"

"No drug that I ever heard of. She suffered internal injuries and trauma that should have killed her the moment she got out of bed."

"See?" Gretchen said as they left the hospital. "Voodoo. Oh boy, what a story."

Now they were in Kearny's office, and Clint explained to the policeman the ploy they had used to enter Wellfall's castle.

"He really thought you were going to bottle his waters and sell them?"

"I think he was suspicious at first, but we made it sound so profitable that he got caught up in it."

"I brought a gallon bottle of it back with me, and I added a little sugar and tasted it. With some food coloring the idea could really work!"

"Yes, but do the waters work?" Gretchen asked.

"That doesn't matter," Swami Jack said with a wave of his hand.

"Of course not," Kearny said, eyeing Jack coldly. "Mr. Dolan here would simply bottle it and sell it, he wouldn't wait around for his customer's complaints."

"If people want it to work, it will work."

Clint laughed.

"Swami Jack is on his way to another fortune."

"I'll cut everybody in—"

"That's okay, Jack. It's all yours." He turned to Kearny and asked, "What's the situation out at Wellfall's castle?"

"It's closed down. We sent the 'customers' on their way. As for the poor souls trapped in the caverns, those who were left alive are in the hospital."

"And Wellfall?"

"He's in custody."

"What will happen to him?" Gretchen asked.

"He'll pay the full price for his crimes," Kearny said with assurance.

"He's still an influential man," Clint reminded him.

"He can have all the influence he wants. We have a witness who is more than willing to testify as to all of his plans and crimes."

"A witness?" Gretchen asked.

"Who?" Clint asked.

"Fella named Kirk. He's supposed to be an assistant of Wellfall's. It seems he didn't like the direction Wellfall's 'religion' was taking, and was looking for a way out. Apparently, this is it. With a witness like that, there's no way Wellfall won't be convicted."

"Great story," Gretchen said, enthusiastically taking notes.

When all the statements were signed Kearny stood up and surprised Clint by putting his hand out.

"I don't like the way it was done," Kearny said as they shook hands, "but there's no denying you brought Wellfall down—and you saved my life in the process. I'm grateful . . ."

Clint heard the unspoken "but" at the end of the sentence.

"But . . . you'd be even more grateful if I would leave Denver as soon as possible."

"I'm glad you understand."

"Oh, I do, Lieutenant. I do, indeed."

Outside of police headquarters Clint asked Swami Jack, "What are you going to do now, Jack. Are you really going to try and sell that water?"

"I don't know. I saw Kate today, and she wants me to go to San Francisco with her. She says that Jim West may have some work for us."

"Honest work?" Gretchen asked.

Swami Jack sighed and said, "I'm afraid so."

"Are you going to be a Secret Service man, Jack?"

"Kate says that my devious, sick mind more than makes up for my lack of physical courage."

"I don't know, Jack," Clint said, "from what I can remember you did pretty well down there."

"That's because I was too scared to leave you people. I think I'll go back to the hospital and talk with her a while. Maybe I can get her to go with me. I could do wonders with a pretty face working with me . . ."

"Tell her we'll be up to see her later," Gretchen said, taking hold of Clint's arm possessively.

"I'll do that."

After Jack left Gretchen said, "Well, I'm certainly glad you're not really a priest."

"Why, because now you haven't sinned?"

"I didn't sin," Gretchen said. "It would have been you who sinned if you really were a priest, but you're not, so nobody sinned. All we did was have a good time —and we can do it again."

"And as soon as possible."

Later, as they lay in bed together, Gretchen asked, "What do you think, Clint?"

"About what?"

"My story. How do I approach the voodoo angle?"

"Ignore it."

"What, but that's the whole story—that and my going into battle with the famous Gunsmith."

"Ignore that, too."

"Clint—"

"I don't believe in voodoo, Gretchen."

"Then explain away everything that happened in the castle. Those grotesque men, the Senator almost obeying Powell and killing Kate, Reverend Wellfall being influenced by Lee Powell—and most of all, Kate being able to leave her hospital bed."

"Drugs, and Lee Powell's own immensely strong will. He was able to control people with a will less strong than his by first weakening them with a drug."

"What drug? The doctor never heard of such a drug."

"That doesn't mean it doesn't exist."

"Well, you don't believe in voodoo and that doesn't mean that it doesn't exist, either."

Try as he might, he couldn't come up with an argument for that.

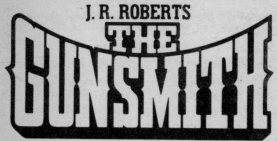

SERIES